THE
RACKET

Also by Anita Mason

Bethany (1981)
The Illusionist (1983)
The War Against Chaos (1988)

THE
RACKET

ANITA MASON

A William Abrahams Book

DUTTON

DUTTON
Published by the Penguin Group
Penguin Books USA Inc., 375 Hudson Street,
New York, New York 10014, U.S.A.
Penguin Books Ltd, 27 Wrights Lane,
London W8 5TZ, England
Penguin Books Australia Ltd, Ringwood,
Victoria, Australia
Penguin Books Canada Ltd, 10 Alcorn Ave., Suite 300,
Toronto, Canada M4V 3B2
Penguin Books (N.Z.) Ltd, 182–190 Wairau Road,
Auckland 10, New Zealand

Penguin Books Ltd, Registered Offices:
Harmondsworth, Middlesex, England

First published in the United States by Dutton, an imprint of
New American Library, a division of Penguin Books USA Inc.
Originally published in Great Britain by
Constable & Company Limited.

First American Printing, September, 1991
10 9 8 7 6 5 4 3 2 1

 REGISTERED TRADEMARK—MARCA REGISTRADA

LIBRARY OF CONGRESS CATALOGING-IN-PUBLICATION DATA

Mason, Anita.
    The racket / Anita Mason.
        p.   cm.
    "A William Abrahams book."
    ISBN 0-525-93351-4
    I. Title.
PR6063.A757R33   1991
813'.54—dc20   91-2515
                                                               CIP

PRINTED IN THE UNITED STATES OF AMERICA
Set in Plantin
Designed by Leonard Telesca

PUBLISHER'S NOTE
This is a work of fiction. Names, characters, places, and incidents either are
the product of the author's imagination or are used fictitiously, and any
resemblance to actual persons, living or dead, events, or locales is entirely
coincidental.

*For the Brazilians I met, who taught
me much; and especially for Peter-Michael
and Ligia, whose idea it was that I should go there.*

THE
RACKET

ONE

1

Fabio was running.

In his mind he ran. It flickered like a cinema screen with images which he never allowed to linger more than a fraction of a second lest they fix themselves and take on life. He ran from words, ideas, certain sights.

Occasionally on the street he found himself actually running, with no one in pursuit and his heart hammering in terror. People would stare, and he would force himself to slow down and stop, trying to look normal. That, if anything, made them stare harder, because a man running full pelt does not suddenly decide he is not in a hurry.

He ran in his dreams, of course. Every night.

He had been doing this for months. He was running, he was on the run. He didn't know what sort of place to hide in, and it always seemed to be the other sort from the sort of place where he was.

He took buses to obscure towns, but in an obscure town everything was known and everyone's face was public property. He went back to the cities. In a big city nobody knew you and nobody cared. But in a big city you might, at any moment, see anyone. The face you dreaded could be in any crowd.

So he didn't go out. This made him feel, in time, that he might as well be dead anyway; and it meant that when he did go out, it attracted notice.

The traveling itself was dangerous. Where more likely for him to be, than hanging around a bus station or thumbing a lift by the road?

He needed a place where nobody asked questions and he could get his wits together. Eventually he thought he had found it: one of the hillside shantytowns where there was neither law nor drinking water. It was a gamble: he did not know who their friends were. But after two weeks nothing had happened to alarm him.

He was by this time showing the effects of constant strain. He was only twenty-three, but he looked much older. He was an engaging young man, who had written quite good poetry before all this started.

2

The bootblacks were back in the square.

As always, Rosa had bought too much at the market. The glow of fruit seduced her, the rich green of greens, the mysterious hues of fresh-caught fish.

(Sergio cautioned her against fish. He ate it himself, though.)

Rosa rested her bulging bag on one of the stone benches, and sat down beside it.

The square was paved with black and white tiles in a swirling pattern that changed as your eye moved over it. Marble steps led down to it from the street, and at the top of these steps always sat the ice-cream vendors with their white boxes, and the man with the tray of dusty sunglasses. Ten royal palms towered over the lesser vegetation, which at the moment was feeling the drought.

Behind Rosa the fountains played, cooling the air. Most of the time they slumbered and the pool was a receptacle for ice-cream wrappers, but in the past weeks they had been turned on at the urging of one of the candidates in the municipal election.

The bootblacks would appear in the square without warning. You would look up and they would be there.

Rosa watched them. The oldest was about fourteen, the youngest did not look more than six. It was hard to tell their ages because they grew up so fast and at the same time their bodies remained so small, the result of malnutrition and heaven knew what else. They were tough, filthy and as quick as bees. They darted about the square, responding to a tiny signal from a customer or a low whistle from one of their own number indicating that he wanted change, or to pass on information. That they did pass information was well known: they were intermediaries in any racket you cared to mention. They were perfect for it: they were children, they could go anywhere, they were invisible, unaccountable, exempt from telling the truth.

They polished shoes intently, as if the doing of it was a mystery.

They had nothing at all in common with the children Rosa taught. Indeed, looking at them, she thought they seemed to be the opposite of those children, to embody, as it were, an opposing principle. She knew she should pity them, but the best she could manage was concern for their obvious deprivation and indignation at their state of savagery. Pity them she could not. They frightened her.

After a few minutes she picked up her shopping and resumed the walk home.

Rosa's flat was her sanctuary. It was small but, having large windows which faced respectively on to a cul-de-sac and someone else's garden, was both quiet and full of light. It was also full of objects. This was not because Rosa liked clutter, but because the objects were inalienable and she could not afford a larger flat.

The most striking and sinister of these objects occupied the corner opposite the sofa, where it was wedged between two bookcases and partially obscured by the wastepaper basket. It was a figure of roughly human dimensions, made of coarse cotton cloth hung on a bamboo frame, with long empty sleeves pinned to its sides. There were no legs: the body was a tube, widening at the bottom and decorated along the seams with geometric designs in colors that had something of the forest about them—a fierce orangey-red, a peculiarly dense black. The head rose, horribly peaked, from the upper torso and was featureless except for two black eye-holes.

This thing, which upset children and many adults, had belonged to Rosa's father. It was an Indian funeral mask. Several museums had expressed interest in it, but her father had forbidden her to dispose of it for as long as he was alive; and he showed no sign of dying, in the home for mental incurables in which she visited him once a month.

Much else in this room had been her father's, in his distinguished and quarrelsome career as an anthropologist. An entire case of books was his; thick volumes in half a dozen languages with small print and fine engravings. Rosa had read a selection of them, partly out of an interest in the Brazilian Indians and partly in an attempt to understand her father. She had not succeeded.

The head-dress of red and blue macaw feathers on the wall facing the kitchen had been given to him by a chief of the Kayapó. There was a matching pair of feather bracelets in a drawer somewhere. On another wall was a single, very long, iron-tipped arrow, flighted with an egret feather bound on with colored thread. The bow was in Rosa's bedroom. A fine earthenware bowl Rosa had decided, after some hesitation, to use for fruit. Gourds, baskets, blowpipes, musical instruments and small painted clay dolls occupied more wall space, shelf space and drawers which Rosa always vaguely hoped before she opened them would prove to contain something else.

From time to time Rosa worried that these things should be in a museum: that they would be stolen, or would deteriorate in the uncontrolled humidity, or be eaten by insects. She had tried to talk to her father about it in the days when it was still possible to have a rational conversation with him, but he had given the high, cackling laugh that infuriated colleagues, intimidated everyone else and had pursued her mother to an early grave, and said there wasn't much controlled humidity along the banks of the Paraná.

This was not dementia, Rosa thought. He had been apt to say things like that throughout his career: mocking things which called into question the basis of whatever discussion was under way and made the person to whom he was talking look a fool. He was allowed to do it because his authority in the field was unquestioned: it passed as a personal quirk. But it was a dangerous quirk; it made his colleagues uneasy with him, and, combining with his combative temperament, his vanity and his inability to forgive slights, it isolated him. By the premature end of his career he had no close colleagues and no friends. Except the Indians. He had loved his Indians.

He had never loved anyone else.

Part of him had wanted to be an Indian, Rosa thought.

A faded photograph on one wall showed him squatting outside a tribal hut with an Indian of the Bororo, sharing a pipe. In her father's eyes was a look Rosa had seen only rarely, and usually when he had been insufferably rude to someone. A look of glee.

She had inherited his books and his collection; her brothers had no use for them. She had not inherited his brains: he had said so repeatedly. "Girls are for marrying," had been his belief. In a row which Rosa remembered as the most violent experience of her life, she had refused to follow this prescription. She had shouted at him that she would not walk into the trap in which her mother had spent thirty years of misery, that she, Rosa, was going to have a career. He was shocked. He couldn't stop her, but he wouldn't help her. And so he withheld what he would gladly have offered his sons and what he could offer easily: money, advice, contacts with the right people. And turned his eyes from the spectacle of his sons pursuing paths that spurned him: one into industry, the other to take, of all things, a naval apprenticeship.

Rosa, working all day and half the night to study and support herself, obtained a history degree at the University of São Paulo. Her father paid her the nearest thing to a compliment he ever paid her. He said she had surprised him.

Rosa now taught history in a state school a bus-ride from her flat. With her degree she could have taught privately and earned more, but she believed fiercely that education should not have to be paid for. She also liked the freedom of working in a state school. Because nobody expected anything from such schools, you could be innovative, you could use imagination. Indeed, since there wasn't much in the way of books, you had to.

She always came home tired. The building in which she taught was a thinly partitioned concrete shell with the sound-proof qualities of a cardboard box. When she came home she would stand for a moment inside the door and let the peace enfold her.

Back from the market, Rosa dumped her shopping in the kitchen, made some coffee, took it into the sitting-room and lay down on the sofa, kicking off her shoes. After a while she sat up, drank the coffee and opened her post. It consisted of a notification of the latest rent increase and another application form for a telephone. Rosa had been trying to get a telephone installed for two years. She used her friend Marcia's phone, round the corner; Marcia didn't mind, but it was an inefficient way to run one's social life. The telephone company kept losing things. They had now lost her original application. Two years was nothing.

Rosa sighed, wiggled her toes and got off the sofa. She had a letter to write which she had been postponing for several days. She had been postponing it because it had to be written in English. She postponed it a little longer by putting away the shopping, having a shower and changing into jeans and a shirt. Then, with a further cup of coffee at her elbow for encouragement, she sat and drafted it.

It was Indians again. Someone had to do it. There were others better qualified to write this letter, and she had no doubt that their English would be better too, but they were all too busy, the professionals. And her name did count for something. Her father's name, that is.

3

Fabio had been on the run ever since Manaus.

Manaus had come as a shock to him. He had never seen the interior. It was a different country. It wasn't just the poverty: he'd seen plenty of that in the coastal cities, spilling rudely out of doorways with its outstretched hand and misshapen limbs, not caring that it wasn't wanted. There, it was conscious of its intrusion. Here it was at home.

The smell had reached him as he crossed the tarmac under the noise of the shrieking engines: a soft, sweet smell, rotten. It hung patchily about in the airport building, and assaulted him anew as he walked through the glass doors to the taxi rank. When he climbed out of the taxi at his hotel it folded itself around him like an incubus.

Fabio hurried inside, away from the dimly lit street. In the hotel room—adequate, clean, Cesar was careful about such things—he unpacked his change of clothes, drifted uneasily in the region of the window, and waited for the phone call.

It came promptly. The client was a German industrialist, fitting this transaction in among more orthodox business. He had insisted on a meeting in Manaus and not Rio. ("Well, why not, it's a Free Trade Zone,"

Cesar had chuckled.) The German arrived by taxi shortly afterwards. He was in a hurry; no time for polite talk or even a drink. The whole business was over in half an hour.

Fabio had a sense of dislocation. Normally a certain protocol was observed, lip-service was paid to decencies. On this occasion, that had not happened. He was left looking at the fact itself, and the fact had become steadily more unpalatable. He was left looking at himself, too—or for a fraction of a moment. He had hidden himself from himself for so long that recognition could occur only by accident and in a sort of flash, like energy between contact points.

Fabio wandered out to see the town.

The smell was everywhere: he knew when he left it would cling to his clothes and hair. The streets were narrow alleys, cobbled and slippery with decaying fruit. It was hot with the sultry heat of the Equator. Above the peeling buildings hung a globular moon.

He found the docks without meaning to. The streets disgorged him into a place of such intense activity that he felt he had arrived at the center of the earth. In the background ships were being unloaded. From that point flowed, towards and around Fabio, an unending stream of bare-torsoed men carrying crates, bales and packages on their heads. Sweat glistened on them and soaked the frayed shorts that were all they wore. Bare feet pounding the baked mud of the path that led up from the quay, they swung past him with their loads, grave, calm-faced, stepping like dancers. Their faces—Negroid, Asiatic, Caucasian, Indian— seemed to him to be all the same face.

This place was dangerous. Fabio scented it in the reek of sweat and the refuse flung over the edge of the dock, and the small smoky fires on which fish were grilling, and the diesel from the boats. Under these smells and the all-pervading smell of the town itself, he scented violence. But he scented something else as well, and it turned him to jelly. Freedom.

He stood there unmoving while the commerce of the port surged round him. After quite a long time had passed, he walked the few yards to the covered market. On every side, as he passed between the trestles and the striped hammocks in which men lay sleeping, on every side and stretching into an ill-lit hinterland which he did not care to penetrate with his eyes, rose stacked tiers of green bananas, growing on ribs that curved like the ribs of ships' hulls.

Fabio walked over the uneven boards, glimpsing through the gaps the water beneath. At the rails on the far side he stood looking across the tranquil, filthy, moon-dappled river. Ahead, on the far bank, was a dense rim of darkness. A silence seemed to come out of it, and a few piercing calls.

He was looking at the jungle.

He turned away with his pulses racing. He retraced his steps to the waterfront and went in search of a bar.

Fabio did not often drink: when he wanted to lose himself, he smoked *janja*. But tonight he drank, desperate to escape from the decision that had presented itself to him as he stood on the docks. It was no use: so much adrenalin was running in his veins that the alcohol could do nothing against it. The choice remained, sharp and simple, and nothing could save him from it. To go back to Rio, where Cesar expected him tomorrow, or . . .

Not to.

Cesar would kill him, if he caught him.

And how could he fail to? Cesar knew everyone.

Twitch any web, and you would see his eyes staring at
you from the center of it.

Fabio swirled the beer in his glass round and
round, round and round. He had known for months,
and managed to live with, the fact that he was a vir-
tual prisoner. What was so special about tonight?

Only that in six months this was the first time he
had been more than a few hours' drive away from Rio.

He swallowed another glass of the cane brandy
that stood on the counter of all the waterfront bars. It
burned his throat and left his mind clear.

In the next bar, he asked a few questions of the
men around him. They were friendly enough, and will-
ing to tell him anything he wanted to know about the
port and the boats. He was struck by their evident poverty and their relaxed dignity. They possessed themselves, he thought. It was more than he did.

He drank, and the decision would not release him.

If he ran, where would he go? He had no idea, and
for that reason had got into the habit of asking himself
the question whenever he had felt tempted to seek his
freedom. It ensured that he did nothing.

Several hours later, feeling like a sleepwalker,
Fabio returned to the dock. He might not have left. The
high-cheekboned men with their loads filed up without
pause from the quay. The unloading of cargo would go
on all night.

He made his way along the waterfront, as he had
been told. Here were smaller boats, their wooden
superstructures gaily painted, their decks and gang-
ways and the quays to which they were moored jos-
tling with people. Hammocks were slung in the half-
gloom between the decks.

Fabio studied the boats. Some of them were making the four-day journey down the Amazon to the coast.

They would call at Santarém and perhaps other towns on the way. Others would ply against the current to the smaller settlements upstream, including villages whose only contact with the world was the weekly boat. In that direction, although the channel narrowed in the grip of the forest, it went far. The long fingers of water reached into Peru, Colombia, Venezuela.

He was trembling. He suffered one final moment of utter confusion as all the ideas he had harbored on the subject collided in his mind. He could go any-where. He could go nowhere, he had no passport. The jungle would hide him. He was city-bred, the jungle would kill him. He must get as far as possible from this place. This was the last place Cesar would look for him. If he did not return, Cesar would seek him out and . . . If he did return . . .

A dull despair seized him, and a searing contempt.

He walked into the crowds—too drunk to care, icily sober—and asked a sailor working on the first boat he came to where he could find the captain.

The boat sailed an hour before dawn. Fabio, from a greasy hammock on the lower deck, watched the sun rise over vastness.

4

There were nine weeks to go to the municipal elections. The loudspeaker vans that cruised the streets of Rosa's town every day, blasting out a medley of popular tunes and propaganda, were becoming impassioned. Giant hoardings bearing photographs of candidates greeted the visitor on entering the town; names and slogans shouted from walls and fluttered on banners hung between the trees.

Most of those contending for seats on the council were old hands, past or present councillors whose re-election would cause no excitement. There were four newcomers to the fray. One was a small boatbuilder who wanted the country to build up trading relations with the Soviet bloc and turn its back on capitalist finance. He was not regarded as a serious contender, which was a pity because he was the only candidate with an original idea. All the others were interchangeable. Their policies did not extend beyond the town, for which they unanimously favored more industry, less pollution, improvements to the waterfront and a new sports center.

Of the other new candidates, Mrs. Gracita Lopes was best known as the majority shareholder in the local radio station. In recent weeks, as the normal fare from this source—football reports and syrupy music—had been replaced by aggressive propaganda and thinly veiled attacks on rival candidates, the sonic battles in the streets had escalated as the other contenders responded angrily by stepping up their investment in loudspeaker vans.

Carlos Pinto, the third challenger, was a strong candidate. A clean-looking lawyer in his early thirties, married, with three children, he had a high profile in the community and a reputation for helping the unfortunate. Women liked him. Men, on the whole, liked him less; he was too smooth. There was also some debate as to whether a lawyer could be trusted. This was illogical since no one would have dreamed of trusting a politician.

The fourth new face on the hoardings—a heavy, square, pugilist's face—was that of Roberto Bandeira.

Everyone knew who he was. He owned a chain of garages, numerous hotels, motels, roadside restaurants and snackbars, and doubtless a great deal else. This was his first venture into politics, and clearly he had no lack of money to spend on things like propaganda vans. He had five children by his wife and several by women who were not his wife, and was described by his campaign manager as a devout Catholic and a loving husband and father. He was rumoured to be involved in illegal gambling in the neighboring state, and was known without doubt to have paid no income tax for eight years.

But in a sense none of this was relevant. The only thing that was relevant was never clearly alluded to, because it was so difficult to put one's finger on it. It was that Roberto Bandeira always gave the impression of being at the center of events. Where there was action, he would have a part in it. Where there was power, he would have a seat.

Whatever the debate, there was no real doubt in anyone's mind that Roberto Bandeira would get his place on the council.

5

This week there was no cooking oil. By the time Rosa got to the shops on Monday afternoon the shopkeepers had gone past apologizing and were bluntly incredulous that she still expected to buy such a thing.

Naturally anything that might serve as a substitute had gone as well. In one supermarket she was offered a grimy packet of butter at much above the usual price. She refused. All this was normal, but it absorbed a lot of energy. Last month it had been torch batteries. Next it might be cotton wool. Once it had been salt, and it was interesting how that frightened people.

Customers blamed the shopkeepers for the shortages, and shopkeepers blamed the customers. But everyone knew that they were really the fault of the money, which each day was shrinking a little inside its skin, and so had to be exchanged quickly for a commodity that was more reliable. From time to time a consensus arose about which commodity was both reliable and a particular bargain, and when the consensus had reached a critical point that commodity would vanish.

As long as only a few articles were unobtainable at a time, the situation was manageable. Indeed what had happened, presumably, was that the things you couldn't buy had taken the place of money: if you had them, they could be traded for anything else. However, when money was shrinking particularly fast—or when people thought it was going to, because in the national emergency which had become permanent the role of belief was vital—the system broke down. This had happened a few years earlier. Rosa recalled it with the clarity with which one remembers certain dreams. A wave of hysteria had swept the country and people bought anything, whether they wanted it or not, could get rid of it or not, knew what it was or not. They bought things they'd never bought before in their lives: statues, pianos, pedigree dogs, books.

Rosa gave up the quest for cooking oil and bought a carton of yogurt. How fortunate that food decayed and people got hungry, she thought, otherwise they might simply stop eating and stockpile the stuff.

Rosa taught because she enjoyed it and it was a job. She taught history because she loved it. She loved the patterns and textures of it, the grand sweep, the telling detail, the freedom to interpret and the iron requirements of truth. She thought it was the most essential of subjects. What were you, if you did not know your past? How could you understand the present?

Not that everybody wanted the present to be understood, of course. The knowledge that her subject was always potentially subversive gave Rosa's teaching an edge. She would have made a good revolutionary, she thought, but it was clear that in Brazil no revolution was in the offing and the number of bad jokes about the impossibility of organizing one had recently increased. However, knowledge frees, knowledge empowers. One day, thought Rosa, the children of the world will turn their backs on us and start clearing up the mess we've made. Let's hope they don't shoot us while they're at it. She believed in the young.

So, every school day, she wrote names and dates on the greasy blackboard with the chalk that snapped as soon as you put any pressure on it, and tried to make them see what names and dates could mean. Many of the children who came to her did not really have any concept of what history was, let alone that it might mean something. It was not surprising: the country scarcely had a coherent view of its past. As a nation, it had a history embarrassingly brief. If you tried to go further back, whose history would you adopt? That of the Portuguese settlers? The African slaves? The native Indians? And what of the many other peoples and cultures that had found a home here: Russian, Italian, Japanese, Chinese, German . . . and a dozen more? Rosa's grandfather had been Dutch, Sergio's Ukrainian.

And if you wanted to tell the truth about the history of the land since it was colonized, whose version would you believe? Those who had left written records had written them in their own favor. They had needed to, Rosa thought. The Jesuits, the colonists, the self-serving governors, the bludgeoning pioneers—together they had pushed the frontiers back in the search for slaves, souls, land and gold. The country was born out of plunder. That was why it was so huge. It had been founded by men of such insatiable greed, such fantastic imagination, that no rational boundary would have seemed to them worth striving for.

Until the country was so big that no one could cope with it.

It was not normal practice to say this in a classroom. Or out of it, for that matter.

Once begun, the plundering had never stopped. Cotton, sugar, coffee, gold: all shipped to Europe, except the gold that stayed in the churches for the glory of God. (Rosa was an atheist.) Diamonds. Timber. Beef.

In 1822 independence was won. Nothing changed. Timber, coal, iron, gold. Always the raw material. There is nothing this country will not sell, thought Rosa. Why? To pay the never-ending debts. Whose debts, to whom, how incurred? Ah, this is where the ice becomes thin.

And why, when the country is so huge, when there is all this land . . . ? And so few own it . . . ?

Thinner. Very thin.

From time to time someone told Rosa, in a friendly way, to be careful. She thought she was. Her way of being careful was to be scrupulous. She had one great advantage on her side. In the shabby, cheerful, underfunded school in which she taught, authority took no interest and therefore was not likely to interfere.

6

The heat was like a drum. Its rhythm was constant: it would get no better, no worse. All you had to do was endure it, and you knew from experience that it was endurable.

Fabio turned his head to look for the Coke bottle,

and the movement bathed him in sweat. There was no breath of wind on the hillside, the gaping doorways of the shacks might as well have been closed. The air danced above the tin roofs.

Two hundred people, or thereabouts, lived on the hill. At this moment, burning mid-afternoon in September, there was not a sign of them. A line of washing strung between a pole and a stack of oildrums was the only indication that the village was inhabited. Even that was motionless, and as he looked at it the bleached-out rags of clothing seemed to dissolve into the white glare of the sky.

He did not know where the people went, when they vanished. Some of them would be here—sleeping, most likely, as well as one could sleep in this heat, a sort of dog-doze which would serve their purposes of expending no energy while remaining alert enough to scent danger, should it come. (From what direction, apart from the police? He did not know.) Or perhaps they were just lying in the suffocating shade, with their eyes wide open. He found this image disturbing.

But most of them would be absent, on their unnamed tasks. Some, he knew, begged: the maimed ones. The children begged, too; and they sold things, little pathetic bags of sweets and peanuts. Or they stole. It didn't matter; one day one thing, another the next. Fabio understood that: the need to be adaptable, to have no prejudices.

The adults, by contrast, were specialists. It showed in the way they moved, the way they never wasted effort. Their lives were starkly simple. They had lived beyond the law for so long that many of them had probably forgotten what it was.

He did not understand them, except for a part of him which understood a part of them. He understood

their contempt for normal life and for all ties that were
not freely embraced. He understood the strength this
gave them, although for him it had not been enough.
He understood their pride.

He did not understand their patience. Some of
them, the maimed ones, possessed a patience which he
found terrifying.

He did not understand their generosity. They
accepted him, knowing nothing about him, and they
let him stay here, in a lean-to made out of lino and
cardboard which had been José's brother's until he
was taken by the police. They said he could have it for
as long as it stood. They meant that when the rains
came the entire village would collapse.

Sometimes he thought that their tolerance of him
might be merely a sign of his insignificance.

He unscrewed the cap from the bottle, and drank.
The sweet, warm liquid, as flat as water, vanished at
once into the parched earth of his body.

The boy whose hands had been put on backwards
appeared at the doorway. He must have heard the top
being taken off the bottle. Fabio offered it to him. The
boy drank methodically, handing the bottle back with
a finger's breadth left at the bottom for politeness'
sake. He managed very well with his flippers.

Fabio met his eyes, and looked away. He did not
want to see children.

TWO

1

The girl at the desk said the airport was closed.

In his first rush of anger, Bandeira refused to accept it. He stalked through the concourse, knocking paper cups and drink cans out of his way and scattering children. And of course all the time he knew that it was true, not only because of the "Canceled" on every screen against every scheduled flight but because—he now remembered—there had been some doubt yesterday whether they would be able to land at this airport, owing to a fire or something of the sort, so it was perfectly predictable that now they could not get out.

The stupidity of things and people.

His own, too. He should have made allowance for this, and given himself more time, not arranged a schedule so tight that everything must run like clockwork. But he was a busy man, and he could ill spare the time to come to Cuiabá at all.

Now it appeared he was here for another day. It was pointless to think about trying to get out by road: the distance was too great, and the very thought of driving in the relentless humidity exhausted him.

He flung himself into one of the flimsy plastic seats provided for passengers, but not of his bulk.

His bones still ached from the drive of the previous day, fifty miles of rutted unmade road, surrounded by a pall of red dust which descended alike on the Ford, its occupants and every green leaf within two hundred yards. Naturally it descended on the animals as well, if they didn't move out of the way, and on the whole they didn't, which after several visits to this place still struck him as eerie.

"They haven't yet learnt to be frightened of people," the black driver had said, with a seriousness in his voice. His face was heavily seamed. He had worked for a local landowner for years, lost his job when a new manager was brought in, and now scraped a living doing odd jobs for Bandeira's associates.

Bandeira had laughed, because there was something in the driver's statement which he took personally. "They'll learn soon enough," he said.

He caught on the man's face the barest flicker of anger, immediately suppressed. It made him feel better.

Well, what he had said was true. The vast swampy wilderness through a corner of which they were driving—except that now, in the dry season, it was a waterless swamp, in which alligators sunned themselves in heaps beside lakes shrunk to puddles—was one of the last great wildlife sanctuaries in the world. Until a few decades ago it had been virtually untouched, a mystery occupying the south-west corner of Brazil, understood only by the fishermen who threaded its maze of channels and the few half-tamed Indians to whom it was home. Now it was being opened up. Tourism was one reason. The wildlife that teemed in the Pantanal, of which a minuscule, unafraid sample could be seen even from this infernal road—the capybara, giant storks, deer, alligators, herons, puma—furnished a tourist attraction no country could afford to ignore, certainly not one that was chronically debt-ridden. One or two hotels had been opened, a few tours were available: one day there would be many.

Not for a time, though. There was a major difficulty: how to bring tourism to an area where the roads flooded in the rainy season and the land became an arid nightmare in the dry season. As yet, that difficulty was nowhere near a solution. The road along which they were driving went half-way to its intended destination and stopped dead: it had run into insuperable problems—the cost, the flooding, the protests from ecologists. For, of course, the road was not helping the wildlife, any fool could see that, and it was the wildlife the tourists would be coming to see. It was altogether a very dicey business and Roberto Bandeira was glad he didn't have money in it. He had money in something else, instead. There was real business to be done in the Pantanal. There were minerals. There was gold.

He supposed it was childish, but whenever Roberto Bandeira saw gold in its natural state he could not repress a feeling of awe. There was something supernatural about it: its purity, its "I am myself and nothing else" that gleamed at you from the rock. In glass cases in museums his hungry eyes had seen veins, crusts and small pools of gold; had seen lumps of gold like brazil nuts, that made him shiver.

Once he had tried his hand at panning. It was at a disused mine in Minas Gerais, reopened for visitors. The guide showed them how to rotate the pan with long, controlled sweeps, taking up water, relinquishing gravel, gradually working back towards the depression in the center where, if gold there was, it would be. The pan was heavy, the work monotonous; after a time everyone drifted away, leaving Roberto. His arms were beginning to protest at the unnatural movement, but he forced himself to carry on at the same pace, with the same care, until the moment when he judged he could spread with his hand the remaining grains out to the pan's rim and . . . It was there. He stared. There, plumb center in the pan, nestled as deep in the hollow as it would go, heavy, tiny, like nothing else. His grain of gold.

He felt tears in his eyes, and then an emptiness like grief, because it was so small there was no way in which he could possess it.

Then he knew what to do. He took the golden speck on the tip of his finger, carried it to his tongue and swallowed it.

Gold.

These days he didn't have to swallow it. He didn't have to pan it, either; everything was done by machine. But he always carried a piece about with him: a little ingot, in a velvet pouch. He carried it in the same pocket as he carried his picture. They were linked, in his mind. Both protected him.

With an effort he pulled himself together on his plastic seat. It was ridiculous to sit in this sweltering airport lounge outside this one-eyed town indulging his temper. There were telephone calls to be made, things to be done. At the end of it—you never knew—he might even manage an interesting evening. Cuiabá had all the appearance of a dump, but he'd found excitement in unlikelier places than this.

His humor began to return, and he got to his feet, feeling in his pockets for a *ficha* for the telephone.

Having made two long-distance calls, he took a taxi back to the hotel which promised, but at the moment did not deliver, air-conditioning, and in which he had spent the previous night (there wasn't a better one), and checked in once more. He spent the afternoon lying on his bed in his red-and-white underpants under the rotating gaze of the electric fan, reading alternately a government report, a company report and a comic.

He had dinner in the restaurant and a few drinks. Then he returned to his room, made some adjustments to his underclothing, and stepped out into the suffocating streets of Cuiabá carrying under his arm a parcel which contained a dress, handbag, wig, stockings, make-up and a pair of high-heeled shoes.

Roberto Bandeira was a self-made man. He owed his considerable wealth entirely to his own efforts. He said so often, particularly in the hearing of waiters, chauffeurs, hotel clerks and others whose job it was to serve him and who would never rise above that station. He considered their servitude to be their own fault—if he could claw his way up, anybody could. He liked to make them feel the weight of it; both the lowliness of their position and the personal inadequacy that justified it. In return they hated him openly, which gave him satisfaction.

He was proud of being a self-made man because in a society so governed by influence and inherited wealth it was a difficult thing to be. He did not see the inconsistency in these attitudes.

He had left school at fifteen and gone to work in a garage as a trainee mechanic. He was the youngest of five brothers in a family where being the youngest did not mean getting the best of everything, it meant getting the least of everything. There was never very much of anything in the first place. Roberto's father had volunteered for the invasion of Italy in 1943 and been shot by a jumpy American Marine who, hearing him speak Portuguese, took him for an Italian. The family was brought up on an army pension and what his mother could earn as a domestic servant. Roberto was devoted to his mother's memory and had paid a great deal for a headstone.

Roberto's eldest brother had drowned at the age of seventeen, trying to surf with a home-made board in a treacherous current. The second brother, Jorge, was an idiot and cared for by nuns. Of the remaining two, one brother had become a taxi-driver and the other a driver on the inter-urban buses. Roberto would probably have been a mechanic all his life if he hadn't won some money in the lottery.

Luck? Roberto was indignant if his success was attributed to this. There was no such thing as luck: luck came to the deserving. What was more, you had to know how to use it. He had used his. The garage in which he worked was in trouble: the proprietor drank. He owed money to the bank, the petrol company and most of his suppliers. Roberto bought him out. Within a year he was making a good profit. Within three years he had enough to buy a second garage. Fifteen years later, by dint of hard work, opportunism and ruthlessness, he had a chain of garages and had branched out into roadside eating-houses and even a chicken farm (the last a mistake).

Now, in his forties, Roberto Bandeira was one of the richest men in the state of Santa Catarina, owning a network of businesses run for him by managers who served him loyally and industriously because he sacked them if they didn't. Members of his family, installed in selected posts, kept an eye on his empire. However, over the years, success and the fact that he did not have to worry about the day-to-day running of any of his concerns had dulled the edge of Bandeira's zest for business. He was not bored, exactly, but the excitement had gone. He could go for bigger profits, another takeover, he could explore ever more complicated ways of not paying tax; but sometimes he fell into the heresy of wondering what was the point. The money went on creating more of itself; he no longer needed anything he didn't have.

He was in this state of mind when he was approached with an invitation to put money into a gold-mining company about to start operations in the Mato Grosso. The approach was made by a São Paulo industrialist by the name of Motta whom Roberto knew slightly. Roberto was interested but surprised. It was unusual for an individual businessman to be invited to join a gold consortium; such concerns were normally very large and much of the capital would be foreign. At the other extreme were the illegal open-cast mines hand-worked by peasants; he wasn't aware of much in between. He couldn't understand why Motta and his friends should want him.

It soon became clear. The big money did not want anything to do with this mine. It was in the Pantanal, a region designated as a wildlife habitat and theoretically under government protection; this meant there would be numerous restrictions on mining procedures, construction of access roads, disposal of waste, and so on. The difficulties of mining in a region which for half the year was swamp would add to the costs, already made abnormally high by the restrictions. Finally, the gold deposits extended under land which some years previously had been declared an Indian reserve. The company would be permitted to drive underground workings through, but would not be permitted to carry out open-cast mining, put up buildings or construct roads on this land.

As Motta said this, he gave a dry little smile.

Roberto had taken his time, sniffing the aroma of his whisky and fingering a cheroot.

"It doesn't sound very promising," he said at last.

"Difficulties can be surmounted."

"Some of them can. Difficulties are money."

"But gold is gold, *amigo*."

Roberto had had to smile at that. He said next, "How much gold is there?"

His companion took an envelope from his pocket and wrote on it a sum in millions of American dollars. Roberto was impressed, and knew he showed it.

"And the costs?"

Motta shrugged and did a few sums with his calculator. The figures he wrote on the envelope were large, but not alarming.

"Bear in mind that most of this is once-for-all investment," he said.

"If all goes well it is," said Roberto. "Accidents happen in mines."

"I'm not pretending there's no risk."

"Good," said Roberto. "How big would you say is the element of risk?"

Motta laughed at him. "Where's the risk if you can measure it?"

Roberto flushed, and felt oddly excited.

As if observing this, Motta drew something from an inside pocket. "Would you like to see a sample of the gold?"

Roberto looked, and was lost.

He had put all he could spare into it; if the truth were told, rather more. He had sold off several assets that were not close to his heart, starting with the chicken farm, and had liquidated his holdings in a distillery. His wife had complained because he didn't consult her. He hadn't consulted her because he was afraid that she would see what he didn't want to acknowledge, that in what he was doing there was something not rational.

That had been four years ago. It was a year before the first ore was crushed, two years before they got the basic problems ironed out and production stabilized. Then an access road collapsed in the flood following a week of heavy rain.

They had to construct an emergency road. There was only one possible route for it. It went through the Indian reserve.

They had already started cutting corners. The restrictions imposed on the company were a constant irritant—limitations on surface workings, directives about processes that must be used and chemicals that mustn't be used—and some of them had never been observed from the beginning. The inspector who came round twice a year noted the failure to observe them, and accepted the Board's assurance that something would be done. But these were all minor lapses in a period when the company could plead teething troubles and inexperience. A road cutting through the Indian reserve, cutting off a portion of it, like breaking a piece off the edge of a cake with your thumb—that was a different matter.

Nevertheless, twenty months later the road was still there. The access road it replaced would always be liable to flooding and collapse after heavy rain. It had to be there.

The inspector, on his latest visit, had been worried. Funai, the government department responsible for the welfare of Indians, had been notified of the road and was demanding its closure. The power Funai had at its disposal was the power it was allowed to have, and its will fluctuated; all the same, it had been known to bite. Strings were therefore pulled in distant places. The result was that so far nothing had happened. The road stayed. The mining went on.

But you could never tell. There were so many influences at work in the capital now, you simply couldn't tell.

The company's operations had reached a delicate stage. After heavy initial investment and numerous setbacks, they were starting to show a consistent profit, but delays in production or a lowering of production would quickly result in the mine's operating at a loss. The company could not afford that, and Bandeira certainly could not afford it. He was over-committed as it was. He was beginning to fear that with this venture he might have made his first serious mistake.

It would be a bad time to find he had made a mistake. His wife had for years been urging him to "get into politics." In a sense she was more ambitious than he was: he would have been content to make money. But his wife's family was well connected: he had in-laws in this and that Ministry and occupying seats in various legislatures, and his wife wanted him, too, to have a voice in national affairs. Roberto had replied, to this, that money had a louder voice than anything else and that very little happened in Santa Catarina in which he was not in some way involved; in vain. She said it was not the same thing. In the end he had agreed to stand in the municipal elections, thinking that at worst it would take up some of his time and at best it might be good for business. To his surprise, once he began to involve himself in the campaign he found he enjoyed it. It appealed to the side of him that in certain circumstances reveled in other people's glances. It was a performance.

He had little doubt that he would get elected to the council, but this, perversely, made the possibility of trouble over the gold mine more worrying. If he was going to embark on a political career—and he was beginning to get the taste for it—he would have less time to devote to business, and at the same time he would have an inexhaustible need for funds.

2

José squatted in the dust beside Fabio, scratching the sore on his arm. "We need a fourth man for a job," he said.

It would not be wise to ask what the job was. Fabio fixed his eyes on the sun-whitened horizon and said, "I'll come, if you like."

He was down on the road, with José and the one-eyed Negro called Santos, as the sun sank. A luxury convertible idled past and its occupants glanced sharply at the figures on the roadside. After a while came the truck, an old round-nosed Dodge with the bonnet held down with rope, driven by José's nephew. José got in the cab, and Fabio and Santos rode on the back.

They drove for about half an hour, skirting Cuiabá and taking the new road to the airport, before turning off into a sprawl of half-finished concrete block houses. The truck rattled down a few streets and stopped outside a big galvanized-iron shed that had been painted black. José jumped out and shouted.

A boy of about twelve appeared from nowhere and opened the double doors with a key taken from his pocket. He looked up and down the street and motioned the truck to back in.

All around the shed were mounds of used tires, of every size and type.

The boy shut the doors, and everyone moved towards the back. Here Fabio saw that a desk had been created by laying wooden planks across stacks of crates. The desk was covered in papers.

José and Santos shoved the papers to the floor, moved the planks and started to lift a crate. Fabio helped the driver with another. It was heavy.

Following José's grunted instructions, they laid the crates on the bed of the truck, close together in the center, then piled tires around and over them. They lashed the load down with ropes, and Fabio and Santos got on the back again.

The boy opened the doors, caught a packet of chewing gum thrown by Santos in his left hand, and closed the door behind them as they rumbled into the streets.

These were not the same streets as before. They had become watchful. It was as if a screen had dropped, making the streets and what went on in them inscrutable, but leaving the men in the truck exposed in bright light.

Fabio knew this feeling well, and the cold stomach that went with it. Santos, beside him, was grinning and exchanging shouted comments with passers-by. Be normal, Fabio thought. But he didn't even know what they were carrying. How stupid—how inevitable?—to be caught on a job he knew nothing about. A policeman watched them from a doorway, picking his teeth.

Out of the suburb and onto the highway that

swung east, towards Brasilia. A bad place to hide, Fabio had judged, with its efficient communications and planned order, and had avoided it. Even seeing the name on the signs made him feel uncomfortable. A tire slipped and he lunged after it.

The truck slowed down on a stretch where there was nothing ahead but a café half-surrounded by straggling trees. They pulled off the road and round to the rear of the café, where a ten-ton lorry was parked, fully loaded and with its tarpaulin on. A man came to the open back door, rolling a cigarette. He looked at them carefully—the two in the cab, the two on the back, the tires.

José got out and made some joke. The man smiled, finished rolling his cigarette, then walked to the back of the lorry and started untying the ropes that held the tarpaulin down. He pulled it over, and Fabio saw, from his perch on top of the tires, that the bed of the lorry was completely covered with paper-wrapped bales except for a space in the center and a lane giving access to it.

Sweating with the effort of working fast, they tipped off the tires, hauled the crates to the lorry and manhandled them into the waiting space, neatened up the lorryload, tied down the tarpaulin and restacked the tires on the truck. It took fourteen minutes.

The lorry roared off up the road and joined the moving sets of lights. Fabio clambered back to his place on the Dodge.

On the way home they stopped in Cuiabá for a beer. José distributed money. There was some for Fabio. He was surprised: he hadn't expected it.

"Of course," said José, seeming almost offended. "You worked, you get paid."

He was in an outgoing mood, which was unusual.

Fabio was a little afraid of him because of his taciturnity and the sores that covered his arms and legs. This evening José eyed the passing women, argued with the bartender about football, and bantered with his nephew, who had just gotten married and was therefore the butt of many jokes.

They stayed in the bar for about an hour and a half. As they got up from the metal table and put down the money for their drinks, something that was not either male or female walked past them. A body, big-boned and lumpy with muscle, encased in a tight emerald-green dress; above it, the square face mask-like. She walked with a powerful swing of the hips, and as if checking a longer stride.

Santos stiffened, looked again and grinned widely. "Hallo, darlin'," he said, and was rewarded with a frosty stare.

"That," Santos said as they walked through the steamy streets, "is a very rich man. Last time I seen him was in Salvador. He sure does go a long way for an evening out." He put his lips close to Fabio's ear and whispered a name, but it didn't mean anything.

3

From an early age, certain tactile sensations and certain scents had had the power of enchantment over Roberto Bandeira.

He knew, and liked to recall, the occasion when the enchantment first came on him. He had been sent, aged about six, to stay for a week with a middle-class family for whom his mother did domestic work. His mother was ill, and the older boys were being kept an eye on by an aunt. Roberto, treated kindly in this temporary foster home, had experienced for the first time the transforming power of money. Everything was easy in this household, everything was light, good-humored and free of the dreadful anxiety that was the refrain to his own family life. There was an expectation that life would continue, and continue to be pleasant. If a cup got broken it was thrown away and was not further mentioned. If clothes got torn, they were tut-tutted over and mended. No one cried or became desperate on account of it. And the cups and the curtains and the chair-coverings were bright and clean. And the clothes . . .

It was the clothes of the mother, and to some degree her ten-year-old daughter Marga, that fascinated Roberto. The boys' clothes seemed to him not that different from his; but the clothes worn by Mrs. Gonçalves were as different from his mother's clothes as—well, as a humming-bird was from a sparrow. And she was like a humming-bird, Mrs. Gonçalves, in her quickness and look of fragility. She was half-Japanese, and he thought she was the most beautiful thing he had ever seen. He would gaze in wonder at her small features, her brilliant dresses, the grace with which she wore them.

He didn't like Marga very much—she bossed him around and laughed at his manners, and compared with her mother she appeared clumsy. Moreover she manifested a liking, which he could not understand, for wearing shorts. But once he saw her as she left to go to a party, wearing a dress of a blue filmy material that seemed to float, and he gasped before he could stop himself, and she turned and laughed. The idea was planted in his mind that beauty, pain and mystery were all connected, and that the point where they connected was a place that excluded him.

One afternoon when Mrs. Gonçalves was out, Marga beckoned him into her parents' bedroom. Her eyes were bright with excitement. She began pulling open drawers and taking things out of them. She took out soft, flimsy things and held them against her, and tried on jewelry. Rolling her eyes at the daring of it, she put on her mother's scent.

Then, catching sight of him standing awkward and yearning in a corner, she ordered him to take off his shoes, and then his trousers and shirt. She began to dress him up. A dark green silk blouse, the sleeves rolled back to half their length, covered him to the knees. Over it went a flame-colored scarf. Earrings (they hurt, but he didn't mind) were clipped to his ears. Giggling, Marga then made him put on a skirt of some shiny black rustling material. She had to pin it to make it stay up. The hem touched the ground, but even so he had to step into the high-heeled black shoes that felt, after the softness of everything else, unexpectedly hard and cold to his feet.

The smell of those clothes. The tantalizing, adult, forbidden smell.

Finally Marga threw something round his shoulders. It was furry, warm and so soft that he wanted to get inside it, right deep inside and be eaten up by it. It smelt of spice. It made him think of death.

She led him to the mirror. With awe Roberto saw his transformed image. He saw in it nothing of the ludicrous. These were divinity's trappings. But he sensed that if he kept this moment in his heart and never spoke of it, he would be forgiven. That was part of what he saw in the mirror. The other part he never understood but it struck him like a hammer-blow. It was that the person in the mirror was his real self.

Thus Roberto Bandeira was a man haunted. What

he strove to recapture, in the adventures of his later childhood, the terrified experiments of his adolescence and the calculated sorties of his prime, was beauty and a sense of being near to mystery. He also strove to understand himself. What he found was a delight intenser than any he could otherwise attain, and a tortuous excitement.

When he began making business trips to other cities he realized that this traveling solved a problem which was fast becoming a torment to him, for although with part of his mind he believed he could not be recognized, he still dared not venture abroad, dressed, in the town in which he lived. But in a place where he was unknown it was another matter; and so he formed the habit of taking a secret parcel of clothes when he went away, and in strange towns he would walk forth, disguised and revealed, into the night streets, to ride the dangerous edge of his excitement and to atone by the terrible risk he faced for the sin of having known Mrs. Gonçalves to be more beautiful than his mother.

4

Three weeks exactly after Fabio arrived there, the hillside was raided by police. They came in at two o'clock in the morning, which was stupid of them because most of the men were wide awake and playing backgammon and those who weren't were elsewhere.

The first thing Fabio was aware of—he was sitting back against the plywood wall of José's hut, half-dazed from *janja*—was the blaze of light. The cardboard village with its lanes of rubbish and cratered gardens was held in a brilliant glare. Round the gaming-boards the men sat motionless.

Then everybody moved at once, and even as the loud-hailer started its pompous booming Fabio heard shots. As the men scattered he ran and crouched behind a crate. It gave no protection from a bullet, but he didn't know what else to do.

The shots continued. They were concentrated somewhere over to his left. There were bursts of shouting, and up at the top of the hill the red-haired woman with nine children launched a stream of curses in the direction of the noise. Even then, it was only when she screamed the picturesque obscenity by which the police were known on the hill that Fabio realized what was happening.

He supposed they had come for drugs. But drugs were never kept in the *favela*; a safe hiding-place, somewhere respectable, was always found for them. Any policeman should know that. Why were they always so stupid? Then he remembered what Cesar had said: "You're the stupid one. It's not about catching villains. It's about who controls the streets."

Boots tramped and there were sounds of splintering wood. Children wailed. The police were breaking up the shacks. Fabio crouched lower behind his ridiculous crate.

It was kicked away from him and a torch was shone full into his face. He raised his arm to his face and the arm was yanked behind him and then used to force him to his feet.

"What have we got here?" mused the policeman who was holding him, and pushed Fabio's head back hard with the heel of his hand.

"Cunt," said the other one, and put his fist into Fabio's stomach.

Lying on the ground as the boots went away, listening to the powerful revving of the motors below, Fabio judged that it was time to move on.

5

The loudspeaker vans had been blundering through the streets for weeks, but Rosa found it particularly offensive that they should do it on Sunday. Not that she had any religious feelings about Sundays, but surely people deserved to be left alone one day a week?

Rosa liked, on Sundays, to go to some lunchtime jazz with Sergio. Afterwards they would go to the beach or to a museum, and then they would go back and have a meal and a bottle of wine at Sergio's flat. They had been doing this for three years and it was very comfortable.

This Sunday Sergio had gone to visit his parents. Rosa skipped the jazz, since such things are better shared, but visited the museum, since such things are better done alone. On her way back, her mind enjoyably occupied with the art of the colonial past, she was overtaken by a loudspeaker van in full cry.

The noise was a physical assault: a blare of music interrupted by slogans rendered incomprehensible by crackling. Rosa backed against a wall with her hands over her ears. It was an exaggerated pose and she adopted it as a protest. She caught the eye of the driver in the mirror as he slowed for the traffic lights. He had a hare-lip. He was grinning, which made his face look demonic.

"Pig!" shouted Rosa, and walked on feeling slightly embarrassed but better.

She had gone about fifty yards when she realized

that he had turned round and was coming back. He
passed her in the other direction, swung round in a
U-turn and roared up behind her like Armageddon.

Rosa fled. She ran down a side street which had a
"No Entry" sign and up some wide, shallow steps at
the top of which a door stood invitingly open.

It was a church.

She heard the loudspeaker van pause, baffled, at
the entrance to the street and then move off into the
distance.

Rosa stepped inside. The interior was shadowy
and hushed. She hadn't been in a church for fifteen
years.

She walked up the nave, shoes noisy on the tiles.
God did not like women, and you could be sure that God
did not like women who didn't believe in Him wearing
fashionable shoes in His church. She stopped and took
the shoes off: not for God, but because the noise irritated her and she liked taking her shoes off.

Row upon row of empty seats. But this place was
not empty, it was full; it was potent with faith and
longing. Rosa grimaced. Religion made her angry. His-
torically a tool of oppression and enslavement, in mod-
ern times it enslaved still—minds of which the world
had need, minds which would never solve the intricate
problems of humanity as long as they bowed to a
ghost.

It had created a rich culture, certainly. Those
minds it had captured, it fed. Her eyes wandered round
the walls.

They were painted. The interior glowed like dull
fire with red, sepia and ochre, relieved by touches of
brilliant green and blue. Every scrap of surface was
painted, every corner occupied by the trailing blos-
soms of a tree, a perching bird, a crouched animal.

Even the pillars, which looked like marble, had been painted in imitation of it, but so skillfully that only a patch where the paint had peeled away gave the clue. And the ceiling . . . Rosa's eye moved over it slowly. It was wood-paneled and over the centuries the wood had split a little, but on this cracked and aged surface the paint looked fresh and bright. Here the artist had painted flowers, and had given them his purest colors: clear white and red on a ground of deep blue.

Something about this church tugged at Rosa's memory. She tried to recall in what connection she had heard of it. It came to her after a while. Healing. An image of Our Lady in the sacristy, which had been discovered in strange circumstances (washed ashore after a flood, or some such thing), was believed to have miraculous powers. The written prayers, thank-offerings and discarded crutches of those who believed themselves to have been healed through her intervention were displayed in a museum housed somewhere on the premises.

Behind her, Rosa became aware of the rustle of a worshipper kneeling.

She left the church by the side door and found herself at the bottom of a flight of stone steps. An arrow taped to the rail said "Museum." At the top, a green door stood ajar. Rosa went up.

The ceiling of the room was hung with limbs and heads. Wax casts in ghastly white, they glistened in the pale illumination of a desk lamp as if pearled with sweat.

Rosa backed out of the room, apologizing to the bespectacled figure at the desk. The woman—thin, in an ill-fitting dress of some dark color—smiled pleasantly at her and said, "Did you come about the cataloguing job?"

THREE

1

Fabio's parents ran a bakery in the industrial city of Belo Horizonte. They got up very early to mix the dough and light the ovens, and they worked hard all day until six in the evening, when they would lock up the shop and relax in front of the television in the sitting-room upstairs. Fabio's childhood memories were infused with the smell of warm bread, the clatter of baking trays and the ringing of tills.

His parents made good bread and a range of sweet and savory pastries. As time went on the reputation of the bakery grew and the business expanded. More staff were taken on and an upstairs room was turned into a café serving snacks, coffee and fruit juice. When Fabio's sister married, her husband joined the business and became a partner.

Fabio was then sixteen. He had discovered sex, drugs and poetry.

With his family's confident expectation that he would become a baker Fabio had acquiesced until the age of twelve. Then he began to think about it. It seemed to him that there might be more interesting things to do. Meanwhile he went on helping in the bakery because he quite liked it and it earned him pocket money. At the age of fourteen he was abruptly seized by a great contempt for his family, the business and everything else, and refused to go on helping in the bakery. Relations with his father deteriorated to the point where they did not speak, while his mother pleaded with both of them and in the end sided with his father, as was inevitable since they had to run the business together. Fabio conducted a silent warfare with his father for two years. He did not clearly understand why, or what had started it, or what he wanted, unless it was to get out of his parents' house, where the worship of work and the obsession with money filled him with a rage he could not articulate.

He had always been introspective, and he had always kept most of his thoughts hidden because he believed his family would not understand them. He felt he had a secret identity. He read a lot—second-hand novels bought from street stalls, poetry, books about history and exploration. The mental world he inhabited when he read seemed to him in some way truer than the actual world he was forced to inhabit, which he found arbitrary and stupid. Moreover, of that world-in-the-mind he could be the center. His parents did not understand why he read and did not regard it as a serious occupation. He could never allow them to know that he wrote as well: fantastical stories for which he could not think of endings, and poems which he sometimes thought were good and longed to show to somebody.

In his sixteenth year this secretiveness, which at first had attached itself only to one area of his life, became compulsive and attended everything he did. He would lie about what he had been doing when a lie was pointless. He would invent friends whom he was going to visit, and then realize in panic that he'd forgotten the story he'd told. He would pretend to have no opinions on a subject about which he felt strongly, and deny knowledge of matters on which he was well informed, rather than be drawn into a discussion which might reveal his mind. He covered his tracks so well that there was no getting at him. Yet he continued to live there (didn't he have to?), eating their food and breathing their air. A parasite, his father said.

It was when his father said it for the third time that Fabio knew he could leave. It was as simple as that. His schooling had just finished (he had done badly); he had friends with whom he could go and stay. There was a world outside: it was time to go and meet it.

But first he would tell his family what he thought of them.

He told them. They listened in silence, to his surprise. It was his brother-in-law who spoke. He called Fabio a selfish, lazy, arrogant little prick and said that if Fabio were not his wife's brother it would have given him great pleasure to punch Fabio's nose long ago. Fabio invited him to do so now, and Fabio's brother-in-law hit Fabio all over the sitting-room, down the stairs and out on to the pavement. Thus Fabio left home.

He found that his friends did not want him to stay with them because they were still living with their parents and they were afraid of the strain his presence would cause. Fabio stayed a few nights here, a few nights there, and in the end, becoming desperate and seeing the thin line that divided him from those who slept on fruit-barrows and pavements, took a live-in kitchen job at a hotel. He hated it: the dingy room, the long hours, the repetitive work, the meager pay. After three months he left, taking some money from the dining-room till because he reckoned they owed him something.

He caught the next bus to Rio de Janeiro: that was where the money was, it was smart and sophisticated. Indeed there was money there, but not for him. It was a beautiful city; it was a bustling commercial city; it was an ugly, mean and dangerous city where you had to elbow and fight to survive. Fabio's wits grew sharp, but he never learnt to work; there was always something in his head protesting that the expenditure of effort was disproportionate to the reward, that work was silly. He wanted to spend his time talking, smoking *janja*, looking at things. So he took jobs but never with the intention of keeping them for more than a few weeks, and because employers sensed this he was never offered jobs that might use his intelligence, and so his cynicism about work deepened.

Then the army caught up with him. Fabio calculated the risks, penalties and general inconvenience of trying to evade military service, and concluded that it was less trouble to do it. Further, he would get three meals a day and a roof over his head. He had reckoned without the stultifying boredom, but he found ways of dealing with it. He day-dreamed, invented elaborate ways of avoiding work and of breaking regulations without being caught, and was naturally involved in whatever racket, sweepstake, lottery, theft of equipment or swindle was under way in the barracks. He came out of his military service with an encyclopaedic

knowledge of how to cheat at cards, a limp salute and
a dislike of firearms. He went straight back to Rio.

Rio hadn't changed. But he had; he had temporar-
ily lost his freedom, and now it was restored to him,
and he rejoiced. He went back to what he had been
doing before—drifting—but now he did it with defi-
ance and conscious pleasure. He hated routine and dis-
cipline. If he couldn't be his own boss, life was not
worth living. He stayed here and there, in cheap lodgings, or sometimes with friends, taking and losing jobs,
dealing in *janja*. He had a lot of acquaintances, but no
close friends. He had girlfriends, but they never lasted
long. He didn't want to get involved. He kept back the
most important part of himself; he always had. His
mother had been apt to say there was something cold
about him. (She blamed it on his father's side of the
family, who could only show affection by feuding, she
said; giving as an instance of this that his father had
quarreled with a brother when they were boys and
never seen him since.)

Fabio's aloofness was part of his freedom. Once or
twice he wondered what he was keeping himself free
for, but then forgot it. He was often conscious of being
bored, though, which irked him because he could think
of nothing he could do that would interest him. He
wasn't using his mind. He sat around, talked (to people
who were less bright than he was, and knew it), and
smoked *janja*. He didn't read. In the kind of life he was
leading, books were an encumbrance. He had almost
forgotten that he used to write.

One evening, in a strange flat, he picked up a book
that was lying on the kitchen table. It was a book of
poetry. He opened it at random and the words shot
through him. He put the book down, shaken. That evening he walked back to his rented room instead of

catching a bus because he felt so restless. Before he
went to bed, cold with excitement, he wrote a poem.

He scarcely dared look at it the next day. But when
he did, it seemed not too bad. There were some vivid
lines. The idea was quite a clever one and he had managed to work it out—well, almost. There was a nebu-
lous bit in the middle. He sat down to tinker with it,
and was absorbed all morning.

Thus he began writing again, and writing, for the
first time, with a sense of what he was trying to do.
And for the first time he read books of poetry with an
eye to what he could learn from them. He wished he
had paid more attention at school. He loved losing
himself in the task of writing, he loved the words themselves, wrestling with them, coaxing and hunting
them. After he had done it, he would walk out into the
streets drunk with words.

He sent some of his poems to a literary magazine.
They came back with an encouraging note.

He was aware that almost everything he wrote
sounded like someone else, but he didn't know what to
do about it. Dimly, ahead of him, he began to feel the
kind of poetry he wanted to write, part ironic, part
lyrical. Sometimes, for a line or two, he captured it,
and that would make him happy for days. He showed
his poems to his current girlfriend, Inez. She seemed
impressed, but said she didn't really know anything
about poetry. She worked in a bank.

Fabio was working, at the time. He wore a uniform
and stood outside a hotel opening the doors of taxis
for people who were perfectly capable of opening them
themselves. He would have been good at it, if he had
allowed himself to be: he had the smile, the looks and
the quickness. He hated it. The uniform was ridiculous
and he knew that the people for whom he opened the

doors did not see him, only the uniform, the servant's uniform. He was looking for an excuse to give up the job. Surely he could find something else? He could do some dealing. He could borrow some money from Inez.

Then one of his poems was accepted by a magazine.

The sun came out for Fabio. He was a poet. He saw his future: slim volumes, acclaim, perhaps even a moderate amount of money (he knew poets never got rich). Meanwhile he could stop pretending to be what he wasn't, and give up that job. He gave it up, and began to spend his time in parks and bookshops, and bars where writers were said to go (though he never saw any), reading, toying with lines, or just sitting. He borrowed some money from Inez. When things got more precarious than usual, he moved in with her. Her flat-mate had just moved out. He said he would soon be able to contribute to the rent.

The next few months were very pleasant. Fabio would stay in bed for a couple of hours after Inez had gone to the bank, then get up, make himself some coffee and sit down at the table. He would begin a poem or work on one he had already started. Having all the time he needed at his disposal for some reason did not enable him to write more than he had written before; in fact he wrote less, but he thought it was of better quality. He wrote less freely now; the publication of his poem had, mysteriously, both given him confidence and immobilized him. And whereas previously it had delighted him to lose himself in the writing, now he found the intense concentration required exhausting, and the completeness of his absorption frightened him a little when he had come out of it. The result of all these things was that as time went on he sat down less and less often to write. He told himself it didn't matter.

He read instead, and then he would go out and do a little dealing. After which Inez would come back from work and they would probably spend the evening with friends.

It was pleasant, yes. The future hadn't quite arrived yet, but the present was full of satisfactions. Fabio was vaguely aware that there was a political crisis going on, but then there was always a political crisis going on, and he had never bothered much about politics because it seemed to him there wasn't anything you could do. He took little notice when Inez tried to talk to him about money. Money? He hated people who talked about money in that anxious, whining way. The only proper attitude to money was to go out and get it, or else ignore it altogether.

Inez said money was devaluing so fast, faster than her salary could keep pace with, that unless he could come up with some money quickly they would have to vacate the flat. Fabio was astounded. He did contribute money: the money he earned from dealing. Most of it, anyway. Did she want him to get a job?

A week after this conversation Inez moved out of the flat, having called him a number of unpleasant names and having said she did not wish to see him again. The landlady asked Fabio if he had the rent. He did not. He was evicted.

Fabio's world fell apart in the space of a few hours. Everything that had happened before happened again, but this time it was worse because he had been happy and he had been on the way to becoming someone. In his imagined security, he had let drop his defenses against the universe. He set about re-erecting them hastily, but it was too late. Everything that had happened before, happened again. His friends did not want him to stay with them because of various difficulties which they listed. They had seen him coming. He found a cheap room the dinginess of which made him feel suicidal, and a job as a waiter which humiliated and disgusted him. He stopped writing poetry altogether.

Then he met Cesar.

2

"Well, what does it say?" demanded Roberto Bandeira. He spoke no foreign language and did not see why he should be expected to. He was a self-made man. "And what did you want with an American newspaper anyway?"

"Good heavens, one has to keep an eye on world events. Our national press—" Motta laughed, and waved his beringed hand in a gesture which Bandeira did not like. Roberto Bandeira was a patriot.

"It says," said Motta, "that a gold-mining company in the Pantanal has illegally built a road over an Indian reserve and the government has done nothing about it. It says this is yet another case of commercial considerations eroding the rights of Indians in Brazil and a stand has to be made while there are still Indians left. It talks about the importance of the region as a wildlife habitat. It calls for international pressure—"

"Oh, stop, stop," said Bandeira.

"Do you want a translation?"

"No." He felt his temper rising, and swore savagely. Then he said, "Who's written this letter?"

"A Rosa Van Meurs."

"Who the hell is Rosa Van Meurs?"

"Well, I thought you might know that," said Motta, looking sly. "She appears to live in the town where you're standing for election."

"What?" Bandeira grabbed the paper, and there it was, under the short, confident-looking letter which he didn't understand. "Rosa Van Meurs, Florianópolis, Sta. Catarina." A full address would be too much to hope for. What did she know about him? A tic in his left eyelid, which sometimes plagued him, started up.

"Who is she? Anyone important?"

"No. But apparently her father is—or was. I had my secretary check the name. He was an anthropologist, wrote several books about Indians, seems to have retired now."

Bandeira snorted. "So?"

"He's an international figure. He'll have a lot of contacts, who between them will have a lot of influence."

"Then why hasn't he written this letter himself?"

Motta shrugged. "Who knows? We can find out. *You* can find out, Roberto. It's your patch, isn't it?"

"Yes," admitted Bandeira. His anger had evaporated, leaving a small hard worry like a boil.

"This could be quite a nuisance," said Motta.

"Yes."

3

Fabio looked fetching in his close-fitting white waiter's jacket, and knew it. He was used to attracting interested glances from customers of both sexes, and usually it was the only thing that made his working hours bearable. He played up to the interested ones a little, discreetly, and sometimes got a fat tip out of it. Once a male customer slipped him a telephone number. Fabio tore it up. He had never done that, and the idea frightened him. Once you started on that, there was no way back.

That had been in his first week. By the time he
raised his eyes from the bill he was writing out and
met Cesar's gaze in the mirror above the bar, he was
ready to change his mind. Nothing could be worse than
this: eight hours a day, six days a week, crossing the
carpet with dishes. Smiling, pulling back chairs, a little bow when presenting the menu. Sometimes his
hands trembled and wanted to tear the menu apart.
Sometimes, when a customer was rude to him, a pulse
beat in his forehead.

He had to pass Cesar's table to present the bill,
and on the way back paused to ask if the gentlemen
were enjoying their meal.

There were three of them. They were all dark,
broad-chested, ugly and wearing expensive but rather
flashy suits. They were eating pasta—lots of it—and
drinking red wine from the top of the list. They would
probably leave a good tip, but they would expect their
money's worth. He had run about a lot for them
already: bread, mineral water, an extra salad, more
Parmesan . . .

"The food's good enough," said Cesar, "but the service is lousy."

He watched Fabio's face. He watched Fabio swallow his anger, to be left with his anger at having
swallowed it.

"You weren't cut out to be a waiter," said Cesar,
and instantly raised a warning finger from the tablecloth. Fabio stared at that finger: he had never seen a
gesture so commanding. He looked up at Cesar's face.
It was even uglier than he had thought, with its bul-
bous nose and furrowed skin, but there was—wasn't
there?—a certain humorousness in it.

"I can offer you a better job than this," said Cesar.
He took a notebook and fountain pen from his pocket,

tore a page from the notebook, wrote a telephone number on it, and pushed it towards Fabio.

Fabio put it in his jacket pocket and the following morning, before he started work, rang the number.

Standing with his thumb up by the road out of Cuiabá, Fabio remembered the telephone call which after ten months had brought him to this sweltering dustbowl in the dead center of South America. He had been afraid to make it. He saw himself standing on the threadbare carpet in the corridor of his lodgings, feeding a *ficha* into the payphone, standing there in his T-shirt, jeans and socks with the door of his room open because the impulse to make the call had come on him suddenly and he knew that if he didn't make it now he never would.

"Cesar," a voice had growled at the other end.

Fabio, his own voice rather high, said he was the waiter from the Lusitano, and then silently cursed because how worse could he have introduced himself?

Cesar appeared not to notice, or perhaps he had never thought Fabio was more than a waiter. He told Fabio to come to an address in the Lagoa district at nine o'clock that evening.

Fabio explained that he would be working at that time. There was a pause, then Cesar's voice, with a touch of impatience, said that in that case Fabio had better come and see him after he had finished work. Fabio, sweating, said that he would be glad to, but he must point out that that would probably not be until one o'clock in the morning.

There was another pause, then a shout of laughter.

"What d'you think the job is, boy?" chuckled Cesar. "What do you imagine you're getting into?"

Fabio was silent.

"All right," said Cesar. "Meet me at one o'clock. I'll be at a club with friends. Give my name to the doorman and he'll let you in." He told Fabio the address, and rang off.

Fabio expected the club to be a smart place where people would look askance at his clothes. To his surprise it was one of the dancing clubs that had started springing up everywhere, and there was a good band.

Cesar was dancing with a tall blonde in a tight shiny dress. He danced very well; he was a burly man, almost fat, but he moved fast and neatly. After a few minutes he saw Fabio and came over. He led him to a table, beckoned a waiter, and left Fabio sitting with a glass and a bucket of chilled beer.

Fabio lit a cigarette and sat back, allowing the tension to seep out of him. He was tired and hadn't eaten all day because of a knot in his stomach. The beer and the pounding music surged pleasantly in his head.

The music stopped after a while and did not resume. Fabio opened his eyes and saw Cesar sitting across the table from him. Cesar's face was red and glistening and his black hair clung to his scalp. There were small tufts of hair in his ears. His eyes were green and made Fabio think of stones.

Cesar took a bottle from the ice-bucket, put it to his lips and emptied it steadily.

"Tired?" he asked Fabio.

The band was taking a break. Conversation was therefore possible, which it would not have been earlier.

"It's a tiring job," said Fabio.

"Listen," Cesar said. "If you work for me you won't be the one in the white monkey jacket, you'll be the one sitting at the table. How much do you earn?"

Fabio told him.

"I'll pay you twice that for a start. Plus something extra so you can buy yourself some clothes. You need clothes?"

"Yes," said Fabio.

"You won't have to work every day. Sometimes I'll need you, sometimes I won't. I'll let you know. I'll ring you each morning. You'll have to move from where you're living now."

Fabio blinked. "You don't know where I live."

"I can imagine," said Cesar. "You'll move to a better address. I'll find you somewhere. You drive?"

"Yes," said Fabio.

"Good, you'll be doing some driving. Nothing heavy: a car, maybe a small van. And you'll be meeting people. Nice people. You'll like them. They have to like you. You understand?"

Fabio's scalp prickled.

"I think so," he said.

"Good," said Cesar. "Any questions?"

Fabio said, "What exactly is the job?"

Cesar's green eyes raked him. Apparently satisfied, Cesar asked, "What will you do for money?"

Fabio didn't hesitate. "Anything," he said.

4

"All I have is a name," said Roberto Bandeira, "but it's an unusual name, so it shouldn't be difficult to trace. It will probably take you five minutes looking up the records at the police station."

"Might be in the phone book," said the hare-lipped youth in front of him.

"Thank you, Gomes, I managed to think of that myself, and it isn't."

"When I've traced this person, you want him frightened, right?"

"It's a woman."

Gomes licked his lips. Bandeira watched, fascinated.

"Try and be a bit subtle," he said. "D'you think you can do that?"

The youth laughed.

"Now go away," said Bandeira.

5

It was not true that sometimes Cesar would need Fabio and sometimes he wouldn't. He always needed him.

Some days the telephone call would come as early as seven o'clock.

"Get over here. Fuck your breakfast."

Other days he would be left in peace until ten or eleven. Once or twice, lying in bed as the hands of his watch approached noon, he dared to dream that Cesar would not contact him that day. Even that Cesar might be ill. Even . . .

The phone would ring.

Almost without exception, the days would start the same way. The first hour or so had to be spent finding out what the currency was worth. Overnight it would have shrunk, but it was necessary to know by exactly how much, against what. There were two exchange rates, the official one and the illegal one. The official one was an intellectual hypothesis of the government. The illegal one was what the currency actually was worth when you tried to buy another currency with it on the street. Day-to-day life was conducted on the basis of the illegal exchange rate, since that was the one that worked, but there was an added complication in that the rate differed slightly according to which part of the country you were in. It was different, for instance, in Rio and São Paulo.

All this was crucial to Cesar's business because, as he explained to Fabio on the first day, all his customers were foreigners.

Within the domestic market, too, the value of money was unstable. This was an inevitable aspect of the constant devaluation. Prices would hold for a while, then surge forward. It was not a new situation, but it was getting worse, and it was essential to know what the state of the market was in order to keep ahead of it. If you were ahead you made money out of it. If you weren't . . .

"Kill or be killed," mused Cesar.

So for the first hour of every weekday Fabio would make telephone calls, scan newspapers, go to the bank and visit the Arab who had an office through the coffin-maker's a few streets from Cesar's flat. Abdul would offer him strong black coffee before taking Fabio's leather bag, counting the notes in it and replacing them with other notes. Sometimes his eye rested on Fabio with a perturbed look.

"You should leave Cesar," he said once. "You know what he's doing?"

Yes, Fabio knew.

When he returned to Cesar's flat with the leather bag, Cesar would take it and go into another room. Occasionally, when he came back, he would tell Fabio he was free for the rest of the day, but usually Fabio was put to work on documentation.

At the beginning he quite enjoyed it: it exercised his cleverness. A lot of paperwork was needed for the export of the goods in which Cesar dealt, and most of

it had to be forged. Fabio was instructed in this art by
Pedro, a quiet boy of nineteen who was an art student.
Fabio picked it up quickly; he had an eye for detail
and could be meticulous if he had to. What served him
best, however, was not his carefulness but his imagination. A bold lie was more readily believed than a timid
one, he found; and a single lie was useless, it had to
be supported by a family of lies that could spring to
the page or the tongue when summoned. Fabio invented people, jobs, life-histories, failed marriages, tragic
bereavements, extraordinary acts of fate. Once he
invented a whole town. Cesar, if he was in a good
humor, would peruse Fabio's efforts with enjoyment.
"You're a story-teller," he said once. "You should write
a book. Have you ever thought of it?"

"No," said Fabio.

The documents completed, they had then to be
submitted to the appropriate offices. Here Fabio did
not have to rely on his own resources. It was known
whom he represented, and at intervals there would be
an envelope to give to the person at the desk. Normally
it was straightforward. He would present the papers,
the official would scan them with his hand over the
stamping pad, and he would look up and meet Fabio's
eyes for a mute fraction of a second before the rubber
stamp was laid deliberately at the bottom right-hand
corner of each page.

Once there had been trouble.

There was a new man in the first-floor office to
which Fabio had to take his papers after they had been
stamped in the other rooms. He was youngish, with a
sad, intelligent face. He glanced at the sheaf of documents Fabio placed on his desk, and his gaze rested on
the envelope at the top.

"What's that?" he said.

He moved it aside with his finger and began to go through the papers. He scanned, went back and read again, cross-checked. He held a sheet of paper up to the light and felt the thickness of it. He lifted the telephone and spoke to someone.

He replaced the telephone and stared at Fabio.

"These documents are not in order," he said.

Fabio's throat was dry. He attempted a laugh. "They've been passed by every other office," he said. "What do you mean, they're not in order?"

"They're forged," said the official.

"Nonsense."

"The ink is wrong, the paper is wrong, the information fits together too neatly. Life is untidier than this; there are gaps in it. I'm not saying it isn't a good job: compared with some I've seen, this is professional." He lifted a sheet of paper in his fingers and let it fall gently back to the top of the pile. "But I'm a professional, too."

Fabio was cold with fear. He had always known this would happen. Cesar had said that if it did he must keep his head and brazen it out. What he must not do was make a bolt for it. It would be all right, Cesar had said, if he just stayed where he was.

He said, "Three of your colleagues have certified these papers to be in order. Are you saying that your colleagues aren't"—he paused fractionally—"professional?"

The official got up and stood with his back to Fabio, looking out of the window. He turned briefly.

"Don't think I don't understand you," he said.

There followed a silence which to Fabio seemed to go on for hours. Silence in the room: outside it, the scarcely muted roar of traffic. The windows were grimy: they looked as though they were never cleaned.

The figure at the window turned to face him again. "Well, let's see what's in this envelope, shall we?"

He slit it with a paper-knife while Fabio sat immobile. He arranged the slim, incorruptible notes on the desktop. For a man in his position they would represent the next three months' salary, and in three months' time they would still buy what they would buy today.

"So that is the current price," he said.

He picked up the notes and put them back in the envelope.

"This has been going on for years," he said. "One of my predecessors tried to stop it, God help him." He took a deep breath. "I will not sign these papers, and nothing you can offer me would induce me to do so. I must tell you that you disgust me."

He walked out of the room.

Further down the corridor Fabio heard raised voices and a door slam.

He went on sitting where he was for quite a long time. The telephone on the desk rang, and stopped. Eventually someone he had not seen before came in and signed the papers.

Dealing with officialdom was only one side of Fabio's job. He had also to deal with the customers.

It was for this, Cesar told him, that he had decided to employ Fabio when he saw him in the restaurant. "You've got the manner," Cesar explained. "You've got charm, when you can be bothered to use it. You've got *class*. And that's what we need, for selling high-class goods. Never forget it."

That was easy. It was part mask, part his own personality; in time they grew together. Directing his energies to the surface he was presenting kept him from thinking. In addition, there was an element of this part of the work that always interested him: it was that the customers, ignorant of the enormous deception that lay behind the whole business and largely oblivious, too, of the lies he was telling on their behalf, resorted to transparent lies about themselves to impress him.

He mentioned this to Cesar, but Cesar didn't seem to get the point. "Everybody lies," he said. "Sure."

Perhaps that was the point.

One of the lies he had to tell them was about themselves, which added another layer to the irony of the situation. He had to tell them that they had been screened, that the firm was particular whom it dealt with. This was a lie so cynical that at first he could barely keep a straight face when telling it. They were accepted as they came, whoever they were, whatever their reasons; Cesar would take anyone, of course he would. Need to believe made people stupid.

Fabio spent quite a lot of time with the customers; part of his job might have been described as entertaining. He made their stay in the city as comfortable as possible; suggested where they might eat, where there was a good hotel not too noisy, where an evening or an afternoon might pleasantly be passed; and sometimes he would accompany them, because for one reason or another they preferred not to be alone.

"We want to give a good service," said Cesar. "Every customer a satisfied customer."

Fabio stared at him. He meant it.

At the end of their stay Fabio would drive them to the airport in Cesar's red Volkswagen. They were always extremely grateful for this last courtesy. He would wave to them as they turned back for a moment inside the glass doors of the terminal, then he would drive away fast.

One of them gave him a present: a cigarette case. He used it once. Another sent him a photograph of himself beside the cable-car on top of the Sugar Loaf.

His standard of living had changed beyond recognition. He was sleek, he had put on weight. He dressed well. He lived in a service flat on the eighth floor of a new block overlooking a park.

He slept badly.

Once a fortnight he had to do a collection and delivery job. There would be a tightness in his stomach all the way as he drove to the farm, and on the second stage of the journey his hands would slip on the wheel with sweat.

Once he asked Cesar if someone else could do it. There were Ana and Mario, who took care of nearly all that side of the business. Surely one of them could do a little extra driving once a fortnight?

Cesar was angrier than Fabio had ever seen him. His language was so violent that after a few minutes Fabio had to go to the bathroom.

"No!" yelled Cesar. "No, you little yellow motherfucker, you will get your hands dirty too. You will be like everyone else. You will not escape."

No. For that reason, to bind him, Cesar had on the first day driven him to the isolated farmhouse in the hills. It was evening when they arrived and there was a single light burning. They crossed the earth courtyard and went through a heavy door. Ana was in the kitchen, gutting a rabbit. Cesar nodded to her, and led the way down a stone-flagged passage. At the end he stopped.

"This is the merchandise," he said, and opened the door.

FOUR

1

One evening Rosa came home from school and found an unstamped, typewritten envelope on her doormat.

She glanced at it curiously. The typewriter was an old one, to judge from the type-face, and the letters were clogged and furred. The address was preceded by the word "To," which was underlined.

Rosa opened it, and crumpled it into a ball in almost the same movement as the first sentence leapt into her brain.

She went into the kitchen to make a cup of coffee. This had not happened to her before. She was determined to deal with it calmly. She boiled the water, put the coffee into the filter, fitted it over the jug, poured the water on top of the coffee, knocked the whole lot into the sink, poured herself a glass of rum and went into the sitting-room to drink it. She glanced at a magazine, and switched on the television. The crumpled ball of paper on the landing watched her like a spider.

She went and picked it up, smoothed it out and read it.

"Dear Rosa," it said. *"This is to tell you that your days are numbered. We have been watching you and we know all about you. Who do you think you are? You tell lies, Rosa, and it has got to stop. People who tell lies should get their mouths washed out. How would you like yours washed out with acid?"*

It was typed on a small sheet of lined paper, and was unsigned.

2

Fabio sat in the lorry cab, watching the bone-dry landscape pass in a haze of reddish dust. It was a big, rattling truck with a noisy engine, made noisier by the fact that the clutch was slipping and every few minutes there was an impotent roar from beneath his feet when the gear failed to engage. The driver was driving with enthusiasm, swinging the wheel and hooting at everything else on the road. The brakes were not much good, Fabio had noticed.

The noise level at any rate relieved him from the necessity of talking. Talking was a problem, he had found after entering on his fugitive existence. When you were on the road, the people you met expected you to talk about yourself. They talked about themselves with a freedom which astonished Fabio. Did nobody have any secrets? He traveled with bigamists, confidence-tricksters, bankrupts, compulsive gamblers, men in love with their stepmothers, Stalinists, Buddhists and believers in the imminence of the Second Coming, and knew who they were and what they were afraid of in the space of an hour. He supposed it was fascinating, but he found it oppressive. He didn't want to know what they told him, and he resented being drawn into a contract by which, sooner or later, he must tell them something. Some story or other.

He would make something up, but since he resented doing it the invention would have a shoddy air, and would be received in puzzled silence by his listener, who would know something was wrong but would be unable to believe that, after being entrusted with such confidences, Fabio would lie.

Once or twice it occurred to him to tell the truth. Of course he didn't. Probably, if he had opened his mouth to do so, nothing would have come out.

It was three o'clock in the afternoon. Fabio had been sitting in the lorry cab for four hours and expected to sit there for another two, unless the idiot at the wheel crashed the truck. When he got to the town with one shopping street and a dried-milk factory which was their destination, he did not know what he would do next. He had been traveling without any clear plan for the three days since he left Cuiabá. He was keeping inland and heading roughly south, parallel to the Bolivian and Paraguayan borders, because the poverty of the north appalled him and he wanted to keep away from the Rio—São Paulo conurbations on the coast; but he couldn't keep going south indefinitely because ahead of him lay the frontier with Uruguay.

It was ironic that he, who had faked so many documents, was without a passport. Cesar had taken it from him on the first day and never returned it. He had thought of stealing one and altering it, but he was used to doing that kind of work with the right equipment at his elbow and was afraid to make the attempt without it. What was more, if Cesar was going to catch up with him, one of the most likely places for it to happen was at a border crossing-point.

Cesar might be anyone, anywhere. That was what ate at his nerves. He had no idea who Cesar's contacts were, who was in his pay, who owed him favors. He had never known anything about the dark hinterland of Cesar's business, from which came phone calls at strange hours, telexes, heavy parcels, and sometimes people who would walk into the flat in Cesar's absence as if they owned it, pour themselves a drink and sit down at the telephone. All he knew was that the web was large, and that he would not know he was close to it until he blundered into it.

He lit a cigarette, then, remembering where he was, gave one to the driver. This further encouraged the driver to drive with only one hand on the wheel.

It also encouraged conversation.

"Made up your mind where you're going yet?" asked the driver.

"No," said Fabio. "I was just thinking about it. Maybe I'll head towards the coast. Curitiba. There should be work in Curitiba." He had told the driver he was looking for work as an electrician.

"Certainly should be," agreed the driver. He swung the truck round a pothole, traumatizing a cow which had been resting in the middle of the road. "I like Santa Catarina, myself. Beautiful gardens they have in Santa Catarina. Gardens and beaches. My wife comes from there."

"Yes?" said Fabio. He felt he should know something about Santa Catarina, but he didn't, only what everybody knew—that it had a large German immigrant population. "I must look at a map."

"You can take that one." The driver nodded at a doubtful-looking bundle of pages held together with string which was stuffed in the pocket of the passenger door. "I've got another."

"Thanks," said Fabio.

There was a pause. They both listened to the clutch slipping.

"Not married, then?" said the driver.

"Sorry?" said Fabio.

"You. Not married yet?"

"Oh. No."

"That's the way. Keep your freedom. I would. Not that I'm not happy, mind you. My wife and I, we suit each other. And kids, we've got three lovely kids."

"Oh yes?" said Fabio, trying to find something of interest in the straggle of concrete and tin houses they were passing.

"We lost our second, when he was a baby."

"Lost?"

"Diphtheria. The wife took a long time to get over it. Cute little chap he was."

"I'm sorry," said Fabio.

"In a way, you never really get over it. But you've got to carry on, haven't you?"

"Yes," said Fabio.

"And there's always something to be thankful for. You may laugh, but I give thanks every day for what I've got." He had pulled out, on a bend, to overtake a slower-moving lorry; as they rounded the bend a bus loomed towards them. The driver accelerated, gripping the wheel, and swung the truck out of the bus's path at what seemed the last possible moment, drawing a frenzy of hooting from both other vehicles. The plastic

Madonna suspended from his sun-visor danced crazily on her string.

"Always something to be thankful for," said the driver.

3

"How beastly," said Sergio. "How utterly vile. Poor Rosa."

He held her in his arms for slightly longer than she wanted to be held. He felt her stirring.

"Did it upset you?"

"Of course it did," said Rosa.

"Have you any idea who might have sent it?"

"No."

Sergio picked up the letter and read it again.

"It's the product of a very childish mind," he said. "To send an anonymous letter is a very childish act."

"Yes, but even so it's peculiarly melodramatic. *Your days are numbered.* It sounds like somebody's *idea* of an anonymous letter."

"Does it?" said Rosa, without interest.

"There's something oddly impersonal about it. As if he doesn't know you. It is a man, presumably. Not that there's anything specifically misogynistic—"

"Sergio," said Rosa loudly, "will you stop *analyzing* it?"

"I'm only trying to help."

"Well, you aren't helping."

Rosa clattered about in the kitchen. Sergio sat on the sofa looking unhappy. Rosa felt a pang of guilt and went to sit beside him.

"I know you're trying to help. But I felt *invaded,*

and it upsets me to hear you treating it as some sort of interesting aberration, a specimen."

"I'm a scientist."

"I know."

"Do you want me to beat my chest and threaten to tear whoever wrote it into small pieces and feed him to the plankton?"

"I thought plankton were vegetarian?"

"Not all of them. You'd be surprised what goes on among plankton."

"I'm sorry," said Rosa. They made it up.

Rosa was deeply fond of Sergio. She also respected him. He was clever, kind and incapable of deviousness. Rosa valued that highly, although sometimes she wished that he had just a bit of everyday corruption in him because it would have made her feel better. And she would have liked him to surprise her, which he never did. She never said any of this because he would not have understood it and it would have hurt him. Moreover, it was unreasonable.

Sergio said, "I think you should show that letter to the police."

This had not occurred to Rosa. "Surely they wouldn't want to be bothered with something so trifling."

"You don't know," said Sergio. "Anyway, it may not end up as something trifling."

He reached for his jacket, oblivious of her expression. "We'll go down to the police station now, if you like."

The police were courteous, concerned, but said that it was seldom possible to do anything at all in a case like this.

4

There wasn't much of a breeze, but what there was of it seemed to have collected in the region of Fabio's table for the purpose of blowing the various parts of the truck-driver's map about.

Fabio gave up after a few minutes and directed his attention to the piece containing the coastal strip. He stood his Coke on one end of it and the salt on the other. He didn't suppose the beaches of Santa Catarina were better than the beaches anywhere else, but the state capital, Florianópolis, was on an island, which made it marginally more interesting than most state capitals. He tried to estimate its size. Not that big; big enough for him not to be noticed, not big enough for Cesar to look for him there. Was he fooling himself? No, he thought not. Santa Catarina was out of the way, a temperate little southern state full of gardens and Germans: why should he be there? But it did ring a bell, distant yet clear, in his memory.

It was two days' journey away if he got good lifts.

He ran his hand over his face. He was unshaven, his clothes were dirty, and if he didn't clean himself up he wouldn't get another lift. He was nearly out of money.

He was tired, too. Sitting there in the sunlight, with a hen pecking at a bit of straw at his feet, he dozed. In his half-waking state the memory that eluded him flashed past him and was gone. He woke irritably.

He yawned, picked up the map, paid for his Coke in the shadowed interior of the café and was blinking on the edge of the sunlight when it came to him.

"You've got cousins in the south, you know." Bitterness but also a hint of pride in his father's voice.

"They're a bit above us, my brother's side of the family. He's a professor. Lives in Florianópolis." A pause. "We never got on."

It was the only occasion on which his father had spoken of the detested, brilliant brother. Fabio had picked up a few more scraps of information from his mother. There had been a row over money: his father maintained he had been cheated. It was all a long time ago. Fabio didn't pursue it. All family business was boring.

He thought about it now, and began to realize what an asset this information might be. Family meant nothing to him, but he was well aware that he was unusual in that respect. Cousins he had never seen would almost certainly welcome him. In any case, they could hardly send him away as soon as he arrived.

They wouldn't be his sort, of course, but what did that matter? They'd be comfortably off, a professor's family. And the fact that they were estranged from his branch of the family had, from his point of view, only positive aspects.

He decided, then and there, to try to find them. He had a feeling it wouldn't be difficult; after all, it was an unusual name. In any case, what did he have to lose? He didn't have anywhere else to go.

5

"It is true that the man works for me," said Roberto Bandeira to the two policemen. "Or did. He certainly doesn't any longer. I presume you aren't seriously trying to link me with this ridiculous business?"

"He alleged that he wrote the letter on your

instructions, sir, and I have to put it to you. That's all."

Bandeira was furious.

"It is not all, and I'll see your superior knows about it. Don't you know who I am?"

Yes, of course they did; Bandeira saw it in the exchange of glances between them. Embarrassment, fear and something else.

"Well then," he said, sitting back. "This is a crazy idea, isn't it? That I would tell a casual employee, a *driver*, to send a poison-pen letter to some woman I've never even met? Who is she? *I* don't know who she is. There's no sense in it. Why would I do it?" A pause. He spread his hands. "Gentlemen, I appeal to your common sense. Why would I *need* to do a thing like that?"

They smiled.

"Obviously he was pursuing some personal grudge," said Bandeira. "He's not quite right in the head. I must say I never thought he was very bright. It was a mistake to employ him, but I needed an extra driver in a hurry for my campaign."

They looked non-committal. Perhaps he was laying it on a bit thick.

"Well," he said, "is there any other way I can help you?"

"Can you assure us," said the one sitting opposite him across the desk that was strewn with papers and ashtrays, "that you did not tell Gomes to send that letter?"

"Of course!" cried Bandeira, almost laughing because he did not have to lie. It had always upset his mother when he lied. "On my word of honor."

The policeman rose, smiling. "Thank you, Mr. Bandeira."

Bandeira shook hands with both of them and walked out to his car, which he drove off with an uncharacteristic squeal of tires. They watched him go in silence, and with contempt.

6

Well, that was that. There was no Van Meurs in the phone book.

Fabio slid the directory back along the counter. "Thanks," he said.

"Didn't you find what you were looking for?" The girl behind the glass partition was anxious to be helpful. Fabio didn't want her help: she couldn't help. No one could. He had always been alone.

"There are other lists I could try for you," the girl suggested. "Your friend—"

"Cousin."

"Your cousin may recently have moved and we'll have a record of the number. Or it may be a new number . . ."

"My cousin would have had a phone for years," said Fabio. He turned.

"I could check with the office."

"Forget it," said Fabio.

He walked out into the sunny street. People were shopping, talking business in doorways, talking politics in the middle of the pavement, buying bananas at a stall. He wandered down the road, picking his way between the shoppers, the talkers and the street vendors. Ordinary life. Part of Fabio, outwardly disdainful of the banal, yearned for it desperately. First he had cultivated the mentality of the hunter, and now he found himself the hunted, and every now and then he emerged from his self-absorption and his alienation and saw that around him were people getting on with their lives and involved in complex and apparently rewarding relationships with each other.

While he didn't have a friend in the world.

His eyes stung with tears of self-pity. Taken by surprise, and for a moment helpless, he stood blinking the tears back in the entrance-way of a record shop, grateful for the music belting from the loudspeaker above the door. People bumped into him and looked at him strangely, and as soon as he could he walked on.

This was stupid. It was a minor disappointment, that was all. It didn't matter in the least that he couldn't find his cousins.

He came to a sort of craft market: stalls selling cheap jewelry, lurid paintings and cloth parrots on perches. In the central space a crowd had gathered. Fabio went to look. A gigantic black was being trussed like a turkey by a boy. Ropes criss-crossed his massive chest, his legs and hips and held his wrists behind his back. He was joking with the crowd, keeping up a fast patter as the net of ropes tightened. Presumably at a certain point the boy would stop, the patter would stop, the man would perform some astonishing contortion—or perhaps he would simply burst the ropes—and would be free. Then the boy would come round with the hat. People did the oddest things for a living.

"Hey, *amigo!*" the black shouted, and Fabio, with a shock, realized he was being addressed. "You think you're in a mess? Want to change places?"

The crowd loved it. Fabio saw that his state of mind was apparent to every passer-by. With anxiety and embarrassment he hurried away.

As he walked without purpose over the warm cobbles, something clarified in his mind. He could not go on running. He was exhausted. He wouldn't find a better place than this. And if he went on he would soon do something stupid.

He retraced his steps to the telephone company offices, and gave the girl behind the glass partition a nice smile.

7

Rosa was receiving a lot of mail. Some of it bore foreign stamps. The postman had taken to asking her about it.

It was the result of the letter she had written to the *Washington Post.* This letter, written out of a sense of duty and with the modest aim of drawing attention to another infringement of Indian rights, and sent to an American newspaper because there was no point in sending it to a Brazilian newspaper, had had results which Rosa had not expected. She had not really expected anything to happen at all.

International concern about the Brazilian Indians, rapidly losing what land they still had to the encroachments of industry, was not usually reported in the Brazilian press. International concern about the destruction of the rain forest in which most of the Indians lived was reported with a fiercely nationalistic slant that virtually obscured the issue. Rosa had had no way of knowing, when she wrote her letter, how interested the outside world was ready to be in a mine company's road through an Indian reserve.

Former colleagues of her father saw her letter, and wrote to her, care of the paper. A few of them had her address, and wrote direct. Rosa's desk filled up with

letters, invitations to attend meetings on the other side
of the country, and enquiries about her father's health.
There were even some enquiries about her own.

Letters came also from North America and Europe,
forwarded by the paper. The writers assumed she was
a member of many organizations of which she had not
heard, solicited her help in numerous causes, and
expected her to know a great many things which she
did not know. Several of them were written in languages she didn't speak.

Rosa was bewildered. She had dropped a pebble
and started an avalanche. It was exhilarating, but it
made her feel fraudulent. She didn't *know* anything
about the Indians. She was an amateur, barely even
that, and most of her correspondents seemed to assume
she was an expert.

There were times when she regretted she wasn't.
It was a fascinating field, and sometimes she wished
she had swallowed her pride and followed her father
into it. But if she had, what could she have achieved,
perpetually in his shadow and pursued by his anger?
(She assumed he would have been angry. Thinking
about it, she realized it was just remotely possible that
he would have been pleased.)

Too late now, and it didn't matter. But she spent
an evening opening long-shut drawers and looking
curiously and with pleasure at their contents.

She made piles of all the letters and answered
them.

Some of them asked where she had got her information about the mining company's road. To this there
was a simple answer. The information, in the form of
a letter, a map and photographs, had come from Chico,
who had worked with her father for twenty years and
normally sent her nothing more demanding than a

Christmas card. Chico was an Indian and lived alone in a converted Ford van parked wherever he felt like being. Rosa did not give this simple answer. You never knew where an answer might end up. Indians, particularly solitary ones, vanished like rabbits.

Two scholars from the University of São Paulo wrote saying that they were updating a survey of the Indians of the Mato Grosso and would soon be visiting the Bororo reserve mentioned in her letter. While there they would seek an interview with the management of the mine, and if she would like to join them on the trip there would be a place in the car. They envisaged spending three days in the Pantanal.

Regretfully, Rosa declined. It was too far, and she couldn't take the time away from work.

She supposed, with all this going on, that she ought to go and see her father, but with all this going on she didn't have time to make the journey. It would have to be another weekend.

Friday afternoon. Rosa got away from school a little earlier than usual and decided to invest the extra time in a call to enquire about the progress of her application for a telephone. She made such calls from time to time, without discernible effect. In recent weeks, with so many letters arriving, it had been exasperating not to have a telephone.

The man at the applications desk said there was a problem. This did not surprise Rosa: there was always a problem. However, often they were unable to locate it. This time she was told at once what it was. She had filled in two application forms.

"But—" said Rosa.

"The computer has refused to handle it," said the man at the desk accusingly.

"But you sent me the second form because you'd lost the first one," said Rosa.

"Oh. Did we really?"

"Yes. It is not my fault."

"Oh dear. Well, that's funny. The first one must have turned up again."

"What happens now?" asked Rosa.

She could hear his unhappy breathing.

"Leave it with me," he said at last. "I'll see if I can find a way round it. We might have to start again."

"Start again!" protested Rosa. "But I've been waiting two years already."

"I'm sorry. We have a long waiting list."

"And you're telling me I have to go back to the end of it?"

"No, I didn't mean that, I meant ... We might have to circumvent the problem."

"Fine," said Rosa. "Will you let me know when you've circumvented it?"

"I'll let you know, yes."

"Thank you," said Rosa, and put the phone down.

She knew and he knew that there was a way by which that waiting list could be magically shortened. On a teacher's salary, Rosa could not afford the shortcut. She would just have to wait for the company to install the telephone for the price at which they were supposed to install it.

She walked home. It had rained heavily that afternoon, the first proper rain for months, and the streets were washed and fresh. The weekend stretched ahead. She luxuriated in the thought of it: the pleasure of living at her own pace, of dawdling in the market, of lying in bed late on Sunday.

She climbed the stairs to her flat and stopped at the sight of a folded note tucked into the flap of the letterbox. *"Rosa Van Meurs"* it said in an unfamiliar hand. There were dirty fingermarks on the lined paper.

Rosa let herself in and stood still for a moment, feeling sick. She knew what it was. She did not want to read it. She tore the note into small pieces and flushed it down the lavatory, put some clothes into an overnight bag and went to stay with Sergio.

8

Sergio loved Rosa, but did not often say so. He assumed that she knew it, as he assumed that she knew a great many other things, such as that he worried about her, that he admired her and that he would like to marry her. By and large he was right: she did know these things. He did not say them, partly because he thought it unnecessary and partly because he thought she did not want to hear them. In this, too, he was mainly right.

Rosa had seen the life crushed out of her mother by an overbearing husband. No one was going to crush the life out of her. Viewing marriage as an institution eminently suited to crushing the life out of people, she had decided to avoid it. So far she had succeeded. This still left her with the problem of reconciling her emotional needs with her need for independence. It was a difficult balancing act. If necessary she would sacrifice the former to the latter. Or so she thought. Sometimes she was afraid she might not.

All this Sergio understood. He wanted Rosa to be happy. It was extremely difficult to want this to the extent of being prepared to lose her if she would be happier without him, but he managed it. Mostly, at any rate; he had lapses.

Fortunately there was no reason to think that he might lose her. They had been together for three years and their relationship, into which both of them had fallen with a sort of incredulous relief at the recognition that this, at last, was the one that would work— was solid, was its own world, a world in which they could move around, and meet or not, and sense the other's presence without feeling shadowed. It nourished, it satisfied, it brought pleasures and intimacies and lots of silly and very precious jokes.

On the other hand, Rosa was not going to marry him. He accepted that because he had to, but it hurt. He wanted children.

His work absorbed him, and absorbed the hurt. He was a marine biologist. It was challenging, complex, and of great importance with pollution flowing into the seas as never before in history. It confronted him with problems in human relations as well as problems of science, for his findings were often unwelcome in the very quarters that had asked for them, and he was used to having to fight hard for a sentence in a report, for a figure in a table, for publication, for funding. He didn't enjoy the fighting (as some of his colleagues did): it was a distraction from the real job, the science. But he did it properly, as he did everything. And because he was honorable and his opponents usually weren't, he often failed to win.

He accepted that, too. The world was the way it was, and there was no point in breaking your heart over it. He was a scientist, not a politician. He knew, as well, that the first compromise would complicate his life for ever.

His refusal to play, even from the highest motives, a political game was one of the things Rosa liked about him. He knew it, and on bad days it sustained him.

9

Roberto Bandeira had been shaken by his interview with the police: not so much its content as the fact that it had occurred.

He did not waste much time thinking about Gomes, who had been both stupid and treacherous. When Gomes came out of custody he would not find Florianópolis very good for his health: that was all. Nor did he reproach himself for entrusting a delicate matter to a stupid man. Most of the people who worked for him were stupid but he expected them to do what they were told without making a mess of it, nonetheless. What upset him was that on Gomes's word alone the police had questioned him. This violated his sense of propriety, and reinforced his impression of a dangerous drift towards Communism in many areas of national life. It was one of the things which, when he began making his political mark, he intended to do something about.

If he ever did make his political mark. Damn the road, damn the Indians, and damn particularly Rosa Van Meurs. And damn Motta, who had told him it was his responsibility to deal with the problem.

If the truth be told, Roberto Bandeira had no idea how to deal with it. He did not really understand what was the significance of a letter in the *Washington Post*, or why anyone should write such a letter when they stood to gain nothing by it, or why a road across the corner of a Godforsaken Indian reserve should matter. In Roberto's view, Indians were lazy, dirty and not far removed from animals. However, trying to grapple with what appeared to be the realities of the situation, he acknowledged that he had to take action and that moreover this time it had better be the right action. He had no one to advise him. He thought of his wife, whose advice was always sound and sometimes surprised him by its hardness, but he had told her very little about the gold mine and he did not want to tell her more now, only to confess that trouble had come of it. He did have one other source of counsel; but he could not consult it, he had to wait for it to speak.

He sat, brow furrowed in thought, in the room he called his library, which contained little in the way of books but quite a lot in the way of girlie magazines, Scandinavian office equipment and tropical fish. There was also a marble-topped bar. He refilled his glass from it.

Splashing soda into his Scotch, he then realized what he must do. It was obvious, but in his haste to impress Motta he hadn't bothered with it. First, he had to find out what sort of woman Rosa Van Meurs was. Know your enemy. Then he would know what line to take.

10

When Rosa arrived at school on Monday morning the staff and about a hundred children were wandering around in the playground waiting to be let in. The caretaker refused to open the door. He was on strike.

He had hung a banner between the windows of the upper story saying that on the money he earned he could not support his family. This was doubtless quite true, and applied to half the population. Rosa's sympathy was diluted by dislike of the caretaker. It was a dislike shared by the entire teaching staff. The caretaker belonged to a revivalist sect and listened every morning to its broadcast on the radio. Every morning he had to be asked politely to turn the volume down because it was interfering with lessons.

Today, Rosa realized with horror, he was going to have his revenge. A preliminary crackling overhead warned her. He had connected the radio to the loud-speaker system.

Moments later a rhythmic screaming of female voices rent the air, apparently heading for some atrocious climax.

"That's it," said the headmaster, and made for one of the ground-floor windows. He produced a penknife from his briefcase. "Give me a leg up, one of you."

On her way home that evening Rosa called at the local supermarket. Cooking oil was now back in the shops, but light-bulbs could not be had at any price.

Life was so full, Rosa reflected, with school, and people, and answering correspondence, and keeping afloat in the rising waters of economic crisis, that there was hardly time to think. Normally this would have oppressed her, but at the moment she was quite glad of it. If she had time to think she might find herself thinking about who might want to send her anonymous letters. Rosa was not aware of having any enemies. The thought that somewhere out there someone hated her, and hated her with a personal violence, not only frightened her but disoriented her, since it did not make sense; and since it did not make sense but nevertheless had happened, what else might happen?

She had not been back to her flat since finding the note on Friday. She didn't want to go back, but she knew that if she didn't she would start to be afraid of being there. She would read a book, and do some ironing, which always soothed her as long as there wasn't much of it.

Paranoia was a funny thing, Rosa told herself as she climbed the stairs. You could be perfectly aware that you were being paranoid while at the same time feeling that your paranoia was justified. But the really funny thing about paranoia was that it often *was* justified.

There was a man, rough-looking and unshaven, standing in the shadows of the corridor outside her flat. He moved forward, and Rosa controlled an urge to scream.

"I'm very sorry," Fabio said, sitting on the sofa and staring at the thin carpet. He wished he hadn't come here: he had badly misjudged the set-up. His wealthy cousin was a long-faced woman of about thirty who lived in a poky flat full of Indian artifacts and broken-down furniture. He was conscious enough of not being welcome to feel embarrassed, and desperate enough to want to stay in spite of it. "I should have . . . Well, I did try to let you know."

"Yes."

She had already explained—for what the explanation was worth—that she had mistaken his note for something else and torn it up unread. It sounded strange to Fabio. Perhaps she had had a tiff with a boyfriend. She did look a bit tense, but then perhaps she always looked like that. She was a teacher. Fabio had always thought that must be the most awful job on earth.

She said, "You must have been very anxious to get in touch with me, to hang around for several days. Where have you been staying?"

"Oh, a place by the bus station." Fabio had been sleeping rough.

"Mmm. Well, I'm afraid you're going to have to go

back there," she said. He had hinted that he would like
to stay. "I don't have a spare room."

She saw his face collapse for a fraction of a second
before he controlled it. He looked down at his shoes.
They had done a lot of walking. He needed a hot
shower and a good meal, both of which she would be
happy to provide, although why he couldn't have got
a shower at his hotel she didn't know—until, looking
at him again, she realized that he had not been staying
at a hotel and went thoughtfully into the kitchen to
make some coffee.

When she came back she tried to engage him in
conversation about his family, about whom she knew
almost nothing. She did know that her father and Fabio's, totally dissimilar from early childhood and increasingly at odds as the clever one progressed through
university, had quarreled irretrievably over a legacy
from a grandparent and had lost touch years before
Rosa was born. She had a feeling that Fabio's father
had once made overtures towards a reconciliation,
only to be rebuffed by her own. "He's made his bed,
he can lie on it," she remembered her father saying as
he held a letter in his hand, standing against a window
outside which a tree was in purple blossom.

Fabio knew about the quarrel but did not believe
that his father would have tried to heal the breach. He
said his father was dogmatic, inflexible and obsessed
with money. Fabio did not like his father, it was clear.
Indeed he seemed not to like any of his family. She
asked him when he had last seen them. She was
shocked by the reply, casually delivered: "About six
years ago."

And what had he been doing, in the years since he
left home? (He said they had turned him out, that his
brother-in-law had attacked him, but she could not

believe this. There was something about him which made everything he said sound like a lie.) Piecing it together, it sounded as though he had been doing very little. Drifting. He called it traveling. He bummed around and took a job from time to time and considered himself experienced in life.

But there was something else. She sensed it, under what he was saying, something he was not saying which, if he did say it, would put everything he had said into a different perspective. For a young man of twenty-three he had a disturbing look in his eye. A . . . what was it? A sort of *bleakness.*

Drugs, perhaps, thought Rosa. But they generally produced a vacancy, and what was wrong with him was that he was too alert.

Talking now about herself—unimportant chat, to put her visitor at his ease—she started to prepare a meal. He stood watching her, leaning against the doorframe, hands in pockets, not offering to help. He probably didn't know what it was to cook a meal.

"Could you lay the table?" she said, handing him cutlery, and turned away to hide her smile at his surprise.

He ate hungrily, from time to time checking himself as if trying not to give the impression that he needed a meal. When they had finished, she cleared away the plates and brought two glasses of rum. Fabio raised his and toasted her, with the first real smile she had seen on his face.

"Now," said Rosa, "you can tell me why you wanted to see me."

His smile froze. He recovered quickly, however.

"You're family."

"What does that mean to you? You appear to hate your mother, your father, your sister and your brother-in-law. Why should you want to see a cousin you don't know?"

He was at a loss.

"You didn't know anything about me. You expected me to be something I turned out not to be. I saw your face when you walked in here." She laughed. "You looked quite appalled."

Fabio blushed bright red. Behind his discomfort there was astonishment. Rosa thought he had probably never been talked to like this in his life.

"You just needed somewhere to stay, didn't you?" said Rosa. "And you happened to remember that you had a cousin. But there's more to it than that, because you must have gone to a lot of trouble to find me—I'm not in the phone book, as you doubtless discovered—and having found where I lived you then hung around for three days until I came back. Not very comfortably, either, I think. You haven't been staying in a hotel, have you? No. You need a wash, so do your clothes, you're tired, you're hungry, and you have no money."

Fabio stood up and made for the door.

"Thanks for the meal," he said. "I'm sorry I bothered you."

"Oh, come back," said Rosa. "Sit down. Have another glass of rum."

She fetched the bottle. He sat down.

"I can't help you," said Rosa, "if I don't know what the trouble is."

He drew in his breath. After a few moments he said, "All right, yes, I don't have any money and I do need somewhere to stay."

"I still don't know what the trouble is."

He looked her in the eye and said, "I don't know what you mean. I'm not in trouble."

It was one of the most valiant lies she had ever seen.

"Very well," she said. "You're not in trouble. When you've finished your rum you can help me wash up."

She relented half-way through this ordeal and sent him back into the sitting-room; he was hopeless in a kitchen. When she returned to the sitting-room herself he was standing half turned away from her, at the book-shelves, reading something. He put it back quickly. The choice surprised her. It was a newly published volume of contemporary poetry. She had glimpsed his face in the moment before he was aware of her presence, and was struck by the unhappiness on it.

"Do you like poetry?" she asked gently.

"I used to write it," he said.

Rosa stood still, feeling her heart jump. It was the first true thing he had said all evening.

She went and sat down.

Fabio, exhausted, past caring, heard her say, "I don't know what you're running away from and you don't have to tell me, but you can stay here for a few days if you really want to. You'll have to sleep on the sofa, though. I'll find you a towel."

FIVE

1

"I have news for you," announced the headmaster at midmorning break. His smile was sardonic. "An event of some importance in the annals of the school. I invite guesses."

"Don't tell me we're getting some books," said Mrs. Souza. She taught geography.

"No danger of that, I assure you."

"New blinds?" someone offered. Indeed they were badly needed.

"No."

"Blackboard dusters," guessed Rosa.

"Nothing so useful. We are to receive a visit from an election candidate."

"Which one?"

"Roberto Bandeira."

"Bandeira!" cried the assembled staff in scorn and dismay.

"What hypocrisy!" declared Mrs. Souza. "What interest does that man have in education?"

"Better late than never," suggested the headmaster.

"Nonsense," said Olga Reis (maths). "It's vote-catching of the most blatant kind."

"Of course it is," said the headmaster, "but if he wants to come here, how can I stop him? In any case, he might get us some money for the lavatories."

The lavatories were shocking. They had been shocking for years.

"Pigs might fly," said Mrs. Souza.

2

Fabio congratulated himself. It had been touch and go, but he was here. A decision vindicated, persistence rewarded. Perhaps a bit of charm as well.

He slept well on the sofa. Several times in the first few days he slept through Rosa's departure for work, only rousing slightly at the slam of the door. When he woke, there was no point in hurrying to get up, and he would lie there under the soft grey coverlet watching the sunlight creep across the window and cast the shadows of the houseplants on the floor. He felt safe for the first time in months. He could feel himself relaxing.

He didn't go out, because there was nothing to go out for.

He read some of Rosa's books, and listened to her records. She had quite a good collection. He tried on the feather headdress, but took it off again quickly because there were insects in it. He watched a bit of television, but made himself switch it off as soon as he became aware that he wasn't looking at it. He felt that if he didn't he might soon become one of those people who have the set on all the time irrespective of what is on it. His parents had done that.

He might try a poem, he thought one afternoon. It was so long since he had written anything, and so much had happened, that it felt like another life. A bit nervously, he sat down with pen and paper to marshal his thoughts.

He had none to marshal. The blank paper mocked him. His mind was as silent as a graveyard.

A feeling of panic assailed him. He got up from his chair and screwed up the sheet of paper although there was nothing on it.

Well, that would have to wait.

He was more depressed by this failure than he admitted to himself. Rosa noticed his lowness of spirits in the evening and said, "Why don't you go out? It isn't good for you to be cooped up here all day."

"I'm all right," said Fabio.

At which Rosa had stopped what she was doing, fixed him with a questioning look and said, "Why *don't* you go out?" and Fabio had walked out of the kitchen and sat down on the sofa and read the paper.

Apart from that, however, he was at home in Rosa's flat. It was small, certainly, but it was comfortable and he liked having books around, even if a lot of them were about Indians and written in foreign languages. The mask got on his nerves a bit, and after the first night he slept facing away from it.

Rosa didn't like his smoking. She'd said that she wouldn't ask him not to smoke, but would he please open the windows and empty the ashtrays and not smoke in bed. He tried to comply with the first two, since failure to comply with them was detectable, although sometimes he forgot until it was almost time

for her to come home and then had to rush around in
a frenzy; but the third he flouted every morning after
she had left for work. It was a way of asserting himself.
He thought it was a silly request anyway, because
smoking in bed was no more dangerous than smoking
anywhere else unless you fell asleep, which you could
as easily do in an armchair.

A feeling of unease came over him, all the same,
one morning as he smoked in bed, and he put out his
cigarette before finishing it.

He thought about Rosa. She was clever, and he
thought she was a bit too serious, although she had a
sense of humor. She often made him laugh when she
talked about her school. Sometimes she looked as
though she had something on her mind, but she never
said so. She had a boyfriend called Sergio, who
sounded a bore. Rosa was always busy. She went out
often, and she received—and wrote—a lot of letters.
She must have a great many friends. Thinking about
this made Fabio feel sorry for himself, and correspond-
ingly angry with Rosa, and when he dropped some ash
on the carpet he didn't sweep it up but rubbed it into
the carpet with his foot, which made him feel worse.
He thought perhaps he ought to go out, because the
flat was starting to get him down, but he didn't.

Rosa wasn't pretty; she had a rather long, bony
face; but it was an interesting and expressive face and
there were moments, particularly when she was absorbed in something, when it looked beautiful.

She was all right. Fabio decided he quite liked her.
Once or twice he thought of doing something around
the flat to help, but he didn't know what to do and he
didn't have much energy either, although he spent so
much time sleeping. He supposed he ought to think
about contributing some money if he was going to stay

here, but as soon as he tried to bring his mind to bear on the subject a deep lethargy overcame him.

He told himself that he was not making any great demands on her—it wasn't as if he was eating everything in the fridge and drinking everything in the drinks cupboard—and that he was owed something in return for the way she had spoken to him on the first evening. He needed to feel that he was not under too much of an obligation to her, partly for his own sake and partly because he felt that, as people go, she was probably better than most. Her bossiness he put down to her being a teacher.

It was a pity that he was forced to take advantage of her like this, but he felt that in a way it was her own fault.

"It smells in here," said Rosa, and opened a window.

Fabio, sprawled in an armchair, glanced at her sullenly.

"I have asked you to open the windows," she said.

He didn't reply, and she went into the kitchen to unload the shopping. But once she had allowed her irritation an outlet it would not be dammed up again.

"You might do a bit of tidying up while I'm out. There's a pair of your dirty socks under the sofa. I don't mind doing your washing in the machine but I don't see why I should go round picking it up. What do you do all day, Fabio? I bet you still haven't been outside. You've got rings under your eyes."

"Christ, leave me alone," he said in disgust.

"How can I leave you alone? You're living here, I see you every day. And now it's Friday and tomorrow is the weekend and we shall see even more of each other. So I think it's time a few things were said, to clear the air. Don't you?"

A silence.

"The first thing is," said Rosa, dumping vegetables into a basket, "how long do you want to stay here?"

He said nothing, and from the anger on his face she saw that he didn't think he owed her a reply. Really, he was impossible. She felt her temper rising, and did not bother to control it.

"Well, if that's how you feel you can leave straight away," she said. "I'm sick of running round after you, and I'm also very tired of your attitude that the world owes you something. You can pack your bags and go."

He stood up and began to walk around the room in agitation.

"Please don't throw me out," he said.

Rosa stopped what she was doing to gaze at him.

He said, in a confused way, "I know I don't do much, I'm not much good at that sort of thing. I don't know what to do. If you tell me, I'll do it."

He went on walking round the room. "Please don't . . . please let me stay a bit longer," he said.

"Fabio, what is the matter?" said Rosa. She had forgotten her anger in the face of his evident distress.

"Nothing's the matter."

"And I'm a millionaire," said Rosa. "Come and sit down. Come and sit by me on the sofa."

After some hesitation he did. He sat awkward and tense a few feet away from her. She took one of his hands in hers: it felt cold.

"Fabio," she said, "I know something's the matter. You're frightened of something. What is it?"

He sat rigid. Then something in him seemed to give way. His body went slack.

"I got into something up north," he said. "A racket. There was a lot of money involved."

"What was it?"

He brushed the question aside. "Never mind what it was. It carries a hefty sentence. I was working for a man called Cesar. He ran the thing, and other stuff besides. I don't know what else he was doing. I acted as his secretary in a way, but"—he gave a laugh in which there was little amusement—"instead of just typing documents I had to fix them." He looked at her. She didn't understand. "Fake them," he said. "I was quite good at it. I even made him laugh sometimes, the things I made up." He said nothing more for a time, until Rosa, afraid that he might stop at this point, prompted him.

"What other things did you do?"

"I did a lot of driving," he said with peculiar bitterness.

He seemed to be trying to get his thoughts into a manageable shape which he could present to her. Or perhaps he had no intention of filling the huge gaps in his story, because after a further pause he came abruptly to the most recent part of it.

"I walked out on him," he said. "He sent me to Manaus to meet a client, and I never went back. I caught a boat to Santarém and started hitching. I should think I've covered half the country. And I've been shitting in my pants all the way."

"Why?"

"Because you don't walk out on Cesar. Nobody does that." Fabio drew a finger across his throat.

"You're joking."

"Oh, no." He shook his head, and from the silence that fell on him Rosa could gauge the depth of his fear.

"Fabio . . . if you're so afraid, couldn't you go to the police?"

"The *police*!" It was almost a howl. "Oh, you don't understand. Look, a lot of the police are in the *pay* of

the big villains. I know for a fact that Cesar's got
policemen on his payroll. If I go to the police and I
happen to pick the wrong policeman, I shall wake up
in a cell with Cesar looking at me. And if I pick a
straight policeman, what can he do? He can't nail
Cesar. If they were going to get Cesar they would have
got him years ago. All a policeman can do is nail me.
I'll go to jail for twenty years."

Rosa said with a smile, "Well, at least you'd be
safe there."

"If you think that," said Fabio, "you really don't
know much."

They sat without speaking for a minute or so. Then
Rosa said, "So that's why you don't leave the flat."

"Yes."

"Where was it you were mixed up in this business?
And are you going to tell me what it was?"

"No."

"All right." She thought it was fairly obvious what
it was. "Well, where was it?"

"In Rio."

"But that's five hundred miles away! You don't
really think he'd find you here?"

"He'd find me on the moon," said Fabio miserably.

"Oh, Fabio!" She slapped his hand lightly to gin-
ger him up. "You can't hide for ever. Can you?"

"I suppose not."

"Tomorrow," said Rosa, "we will go out." He
flinched. "Yes we will. The longer you stay here cooped
up, the harder it will be for you to go out. You were
all right last week, when you got here, weren't you,
walking around?"

"Yes, but then I'd only just arrived. He wouldn't
have had time . . ."

"Mmm. I can see that we have to do something

about it quickly. We'll go to the beach, if it's fine, and perhaps we'll have lunch somewhere, and we might even see a film ... Yes, and meanwhile," said Rosa, standing up, "I'll make something to eat."

She stopped half-way to the kitchen. "I have an even better idea. You can make something to eat."

There was an appalled silence. "But I can't cook, except things out of tins," said Fabio after a while.

"I'll teach you. It's quite easy. Everybody should be able to cook. Come here and I'll show you how to chop an onion."

He came to the kitchen, an unwilling, sheepish, pleased grin on his face. He would be all right, Rosa thought. He would not be the first she'd rescued. Sometimes she wished somebody would ask if *she* needed help, but that was the way it was. Those who were capable were presumed to be capable for all time.

"There is something I ought to say, Fabio," she said, knife poised over the veined globe, "and that is that I can't afford to keep you. You'll have to look for a job."

The expression on his face was so pitiful that she giggled. Then an idea came to her, and her mirth increased. "I know the very thing. There's a church not far from here which has a museum of votive offerings: arms and legs made out of wax, and paintings of shipwrecks being prevented by divine intervention, and much more in the same line. They want someone to catalogue the collection. I think it would suit you down to the ground."

3

The day of Roberto Bandeira's visit arrived.

The caretaker, to the silent fury of the teaching staff, had hung a red-and-white banner (the candi-

date's colors) across the entrance. He was evidently a
Bandeira man. Beneath this banner the headmaster
and his senior teachers stood to await their guest.

He was fifteen minutes late. When he came, the
long-nosed gray car he drove (it was a foible of his not
to employ a chauffeur) was accompanied by two others. In the motorcade were Bandeira's wife and eldest
daughter, his male secretary, two Japanese business
associates and four thickset men with short haircuts
whose eyes darted everywhere. This party, welcomed
by the headmaster, moved down the corridor in a
block and entered the staffroom, which, when the
headmaster had taken up his position by the coffee
cups, it more or less filled.

"Not much room in here, is there?" chuckled Bandeira, running his eyes over the cracked plaster of the
ceiling, and holding his cup in a hand that looked like
the paw of a bulldozer.

He was introduced to the staff in turn. When he
came to Rosa he prolonged the handshake for what
seemed to her a long time, while looking into her eyes.
Rosa was embarrassed: it was remarkably indiscreet
behavior with his wife and daughter present. But perhaps they were used to it? She found him repulsive
and wished he would move on to Olga Reis, who was
standing at her elbow, but Olga was angular and forty-
three and he showed no inclination to do so.

He enquired, with an interest she knew he could
not feel, about the methods of teaching history and
how she viewed the task of a teacher. History lessons
in his youth, he said, had been mainly a question of
reciting dates and the names of kings.

Rosa smiled. "There's not so much of that now,
I'm glad to say."

He said he was charmed to have met her, and that

if she had any problems she must not hesitate to get in touch with him. Then, at last, he transferred his attention to Olga, leaving Rosa perplexed as to what problems she might ever have with which Roberto Bandeira could be of assistance, and aware, across the small room, of the cold stare of his daughter.

After coffee the party toured the classrooms. Bandeira asked the children how they liked school. A few of them, the politer ones, attempted a reply. Most of them simply stared at him, at his wife's eleven bangles, at the twin-faced Japanese business associates and the four men with short haircuts who entered every room as if to surround its occupants.

He told the children how much he had enjoyed his own schooldays, which was so patent a lie that their eyes widened at it. He asked the teachers if he could see the books they used, and seemed disconcerted when shown the small, tattered stock of the school's teaching materials.

In the class which Rosa was taking he asked some elementary questions and, having ascertained from his wife that the answers were correct, professed satisfaction. He said, in front of Mrs. Souza's frankly incredulous geography class, that the mineral wealth of Brazil would make it the richest country in the world within the next quarter of a century.

After an hour and a half in which normal work had been impossible, Roberto Bandeira led his party to the main entrance, delivered himself of a short speech on the importance of education to the country's future, and departed.

Flanked by his senior staff, the headmaster watched him go.

"*Is* he going to get us any money?" asked Mrs. Souza.

"Yes," said the headmaster. "He's going to give us the money to enlarge the staffroom."

"How can we do that?"

"He suggests we knock a hole through the wall into the broom cupboard."

4

It was a tremendous relief to confide in someone. It was like coming out of prison.

Fabio was surprised and a little shaken at what had happened in his conversation with Rosa. He had never opened himself up to anyone to that extent before; he did not like people to get too near him. He was afraid of the demands they would make on him, and that if they knew much about him they would not respect him; and also that it would in some way weaken him, as if his strength lay in his silence.

He had labored along, under his gradually increasing burden, without realizing how simple it would be to put it down, and how heavy it had become.

Putting it down was so pleasant and invigorating that he would have liked to do it again, but Rosa was always busy or the moment was wrong and he didn't know how to start. Nor, in fact, did he have a clear idea what he wanted to say. He just wanted to talk to her again; to talk about himself; to feel her attention on him.

It was dangerous, he realized that. He had been right to think that if you let people get close to you they could hurt you, because he had been wounded by Rosa's withdrawal of interest after the end of the conversation, her assumption that life would go on as before, the only difference being that now there was a

larger area that could be talked about. He had expected that now he had shown her—as it were—who
he was, she would treat him somehow differently. She
treated him in exactly the same way as before, and she
expected him to get a job.

At first, because she laughed when talking about
it, he had thought the business about the cataloguing
at the church was a joke, but then a couple of days
later she asked him if he had done anything about it.
Surprised (and hurt), Fabio had said no. Rosa had not
expressed annoyance, she had merely said, "Well, why
don't you go along there tomorrow?" but in the
moment before she said it there had come into her eyes
a look of patience which Fabio had seen before, in the
eyes of other women, starting with his mother.

Fabio noticed, and resented it.

But, because he did want to go on staying there
and because he had begun to realize that Rosa always
meant what she said, he went to the church to enquire
about the cataloguing job.

"Yes, dear?" said the woman at the desk by the
door. She was wearing a black dress with gray flowers
printed on it, and a cameo brooch surrounded with
imitation diamonds. Her hair was pulled back from
her face and tied in a bun. She wore spectacles with
pink frames and her face was the color of pastry dough.
She reminded Fabio of a great-aunt he had disliked.
However, she was smiling agreeably, which his great-
aunt had never done.

"I was told you were looking for someone to catalogue the collection," said Fabio.

He had glanced around as he came in. It was like
a cross between a mortuary and a doll's house. Despite
himself, he felt a prickling of curiosity.

"Do you want to apply, dear?"

"Yes," said Fabio.

"Have you done this sort of work before?"

"Well," said Fabio, "in Rio I had to . . . er, catalogue documents for a businessman."

"I see. This is rather a different kind of thing. You
are . . ." She hesitated. "You do *believe*, do you?"

"Oh yes," said Fabio.

"Father Luigi insists on a Catholic. We did appoint
somebody, but he proved rather unreliable." She lowered her voice. "He *drank*. He hasn't been back for a
week, and frankly I can't say I'm sorry, but meanwhile
the work isn't getting done. And we have to vacate this
room in three months' time because of the restoration
work and the collection *must* be catalogued by then.
And I can't do it, I have my hands full at the desk."

On the desk were a visitors' book, a cash box, a
table lamp in the shape of a mermaid and a novel.

"Would you like to look at the collection?" she
asked, rising from her chair.

"Yes, please," said Fabio.

For half an hour he peered into glass cases containing macabre objects, and dusty corners where
reposed cast-off surgical appliances, motorcycle helmets and pictures in broken frames. Ducking his head
at the end of this tour to avoid the feet hanging from
the ceiling, he bumped it against a low-flying tin airplane; and, pausing to steady the latter on its wire, he
found himself staring at the human-size model of a bee
in cellophane and velvet, its transparent wings outspread, its huge eyes of mirror-glass winking.

"The gem of the collection," said his guide. "A little girl, badly stung by bees and at the point of death.
Her father made it. Beautiful, isn't it? Alas, most of
our exhibits aren't in anything like such a good state
of repair. Between ourselves"—she shook her head over

a pile of something or other moldering under a bench—"it's not only cataloguing that's needed."

They returned to the desk.

"Well," she said, "are you still interested?"

"How much are you paying?" asked Fabio, and it wasn't much. But then, it was only round the corner, and Cesar would never find him there, and in any case he wasn't doing it for the money, he was doing it to keep Rosa quiet. It wasn't even that. He had been either frightened out of his wits or bored out of his mind for as long as he could remember, and in this museum of the grotesque he found something that both tickled his imagination and harmonized with his mood.

"Yes, I'd like to apply," he said.

"Good," she said. "I am Mrs. Cruz. And you?"

"Felipe," he answered unhesitatingly. "Felipe da Silva."

5

Rosa's doorbell rang, purposefully, at seven o'clock that evening. Rosa was in the bathroom getting ready to go out. She called to Fabio to ask him to answer the door.

"I can't," protested Fabio. He never answered the door. He thought it was understood between them that he should never have to.

"Oh, Fabio, please!" begged Rosa.

Grumbling, Fabio went. Outside the door stood two policemen.

Fabio had various options, and nearly took the wrong one. If he had dashed for the stairway they would probably have shot him. Before he could com-

mit suicide, one of the policemen said, "Does Rosa Van
Meurs live here?"

Fabio grappled with, and grasped in time, the idea
that they did not want him. Then as he stood there,
still hesitating, wanting to protect Rosa from whatever
it was that threatened, Rosa's clear voice came from
the bathroom again, asking who was there. The policemen, without waiting for a further invitation, walked
past Fabio and stood in the hallway.

"Police, Miss Van Meurs," said the older one.
"Regarding your visit to the station on the sixteenth."

There was a protracted clatter, and Rosa emerged,
looking startled.

"Yes, what is it?"

"We have some news for you, Miss. Would you like
to come down to the station?"

"Yes, of course," said Rosa, and as Fabio watched,
bewildered and obscurely put out, she picked up a
jumper and went with them.

Rosa had known what it was as soon as she heard
their voices. In the car they confirmed it. They had
found the man who had written the anonymous letter.
They told her his name; it meant nothing.

Rosa found herself smiling. She felt lighter, physically lighter. They had caught him: there would be no
more letters. Equally important was that the letter was
proved to have been written by a real person; it was
not some incomprehensible demonic irruption into her
life, or a manifestation of her own unconscious. As for
who had written it, she was oddly incurious. It was
someone mad. That made it unlikely that she knew
him, and irrelevant whether he thought he knew her.

But she did know him. She stared at the hare-
lipped face in the photograph which they put before
her at the station, unable to recall where she had seen

it. She said, at last, that she couldn't place him, but that she knew she had never spoken to him.

"You're sure of that?"

"Quite sure," said Rosa.

The policemen exchanged a look which she couldn't read.

"Have you charged him?" she asked.

"There's nothing really we can charge him with," said the senior one. "All we can do is give him a little fright. If it was a personal grudge it would be a different matter. We might have to do something then, because these cases can turn nasty. But he says he doesn't know you, and you've confirmed that. It appears he just picked your name out of the phone book."

"I'm not in the phone book."

"A street directory," said the other policeman.

"That's right," said the senior one.

"But why?" said Rosa.

The younger policeman tapped his forehead.

"He won't . . . do it again?" ventured Rosa.

They both laughed. "Oh no, Miss. He won't do it again."

Rosa was puzzled. There was something they weren't telling her. But they were policemen and they didn't have to tell her anything at all. She realized they had been kind: it was a trivial matter and they had wanted to set her mind at rest.

"Thank you," she said. "Thank you very much."

After she left the station she wondered how on earth they had found him, and wished she'd asked.

SIX

1

"What progress have you made?" asked Motta on a bad line from São Paulo. "It's ten days since I heard from you."

Motta always put him on the defensive. Bandeira resented this but for a variety of reasons was unable to deal with it.

"I put a man on to it," he said, thankful that this was a telephone conversation and he could not be expected to be explicit.

"So you said before. Was he successful?"

Bandeira was silent too long.

"Roberto, can you hear me? This is a bad line, your voice keeps fading."

"I'll ring you back," said Bandeira quickly.

"No, no, I can hear you now. I said, was your man successful?"

"Well, no, not completely I'm afraid. But I've now taken charge of things myself."

"What d'you mean?"

"I've met the person concerned."

"How enterprising. What did you mean when you said 'not completely successful?' You mean he made a balls-up of it?"

"It's difficult to discuss this over the phone," said Bandeira. "Can we arrange a meeting?"

"If you like, but you'll have to come to São Paulo. I'm very tied up at the moment."

"All right," said Bandeira, annoyed. "Give me a few more days. Then I should have something positive to report."

"Well, I hope you will. Time's passing, Roberto. You realize that letter started a whole correspondence?"

"What?"

"You should read the foreign press." Cruelly: "Or get someone to read it to you."

"I don't have much time for reading," said Bandeira. "I have businesses to run."

"Don't we all? You say you'll have something to report in a few days?"

"That's right."

"You'll get in touch with me, then?"

"Yes," said Bandeira, conscious that it was a directive and not a question.

"Good," said Motta, and rang off.

Bandeira was anxious as he put the phone down. It was true he had a trick up his sleeve, but it was a very tricky trick. He would rather not have been pushed into playing it, and he wasn't sure it would work.

2

Rosa received a letter with a Canadian stamp. She read it and her coffee went cold.

It informed her that a conference under the auspices of Survival International, to discuss the threat to the world's remaining tribal peoples, was to be held in Toronto in two months' time. Rosa was aware of this fact: several of her correspondents outside Latin America had mentioned it and asked if she would be there, causing Rosa to smile dryly at the innocence of First-World academics.

The letter was an invitation to attend the conference as an observer. It said that accommodation would be found for her, if she wished, in the home of one of the Toronto delegates. She would have to pay her own air fare, of course.

Rosa's foreign travel had been limited to a week in Argentina with her friend Marcia when they were both students. She had imagined that, barring miracles, it always would be.

Head whirling, she went into a travel agency and enquired the air fare to Toronto. She came out feeling steadier. It was completely out of the question.

"I'll lend you the money," offered Sergio.

"You haven't got it." Sergio's pay was chronically in arrears, for a reason no one seemed able to find out.

"No, but my father has."

Sergio's father had invented something, Rosa could never remember what. He spent only a small percentage of the royalties. He did not seem to know what to do with money. He was not, on the other hand, generous with it.

"He never gives you any," noted Rosa.

"Oh, that's because I'm his son. But he'd lend it to you. He likes you."

Indeed they liked each other.

Rosa thought about it for a few vivid hours. Then she thanked Sergio and said no.

"I don't know how I'd pay it back, for one thing."

"You could take as long as you like to pay it back. He doesn't need it."

"All the same, no."

"Why not?"

"Because."

It didn't matter. After a day or so she was quite content not to be going. It would have been an adventure, but she knew that in spite of its serious guise it was a frivolous idea. Only a small part of the conference agenda would be concerned with Indians, and if she wanted to find out about Indians the best place to start was her sitting-room. She would have liked to meet some of the people who had written to her; but perhaps one day she would, and meanwhile she could keep in touch with them.

Somewhere ahead of her, Rosa sensed a change in her life. It was going to broaden out, become freer, more active. She was impatient for the change, but had a strong feeling that there was nothing she could do, because whatever it was wasn't ready yet.

She hoped she would be ready for it, when it came.

She wondered how long Fabio would stay in the flat. Not much longer, presumably.

3

Rosa's headmaster was surprised to receive a notification that the school would shortly be visited by an inspector. No inspector had visited the school for

years. He could not decide whether it boded good
or ill.

"Ill," said Mrs. Souza. She had been teaching for
thirty years, and had seen most things.

4

Although he did not have to be at the museum until
ten o'clock, Fabio got up at the same time as Rosa
every morning. He did so because he knew that if he
didn't he would have difficulty in getting up at all. He
vaguely expected, on the first morning, that Rosa
would make breakfast for both of them, but when he
popped his head round the kitchen door she was standing there with one shoe on and one shoe off, eating a
piece of bread and jam with one hand and putting
books into a briefcase with the other. She pushed the
loaf towards him, put on her other shoe, said, "See you
this evening," and left. Fabio got his own breakfast.

For the next two mornings they circled round each
other, cutting and eating pieces of bread and trying
not to knock over each other's coffee. Then an idea
came to Fabio. One morning he got to the kitchen
before Rosa, and made breakfast. When Rosa emerged
from the bathroom it was on the table: coffee, bread,
jam and two eggs.

Rosa stopped half-way across the carpet in astonishment. Then a smile lit up her face. "That's nice,"
she said.

Pleased with the effect, Fabio made breakfast on
succeeding mornings. After a week it was a chore. He
said dejectedly, "Do you want me to make breakfast
every day?"

Rosa seemed to find this very amusing. When she

had finished laughing, she said, "I don't normally sit down to breakfast except at weekends."

"Don't you like breakfast?"

"I don't usually have time."

Fabio was hurt. He understood, of course: her priority in the morning was to get to work; but it still felt like a rejection of his gift. He wanted, in retaliation, not to do the washing up, which he now did as a contribution to the housework; but he thought that if he didn't she would think he was being childish, after which it occurred to him that he was being childish, so he got on and did it. They settled down to an arrangement in which sometimes there was and sometimes there wasn't breakfast.

Rosa was difficult to get to know, Fabio concluded. It had taken him a while to realize this because of the openness of her manner. The openness was genuine, but some way behind it lay a privacy which almost matched his own. He suspected that he knew next to nothing about what really went on in Rosa's life. She didn't talk about Sergio, or at least not in the way he expected a woman to talk about her man friend. From letters which she left lying about (he half-read a few; he was ashamed to read them through to the end) it appeared she was involved in something to do with Indians, but she never talked about that either. And there was the unexplained visit of the two policemen.

Fabio knew a blameless life when he saw one, but he nevertheless wondered if Rosa was in some sort of trouble. Several times at the beginning of his stay he had surprised a worried and apprehensive look on her face. He hadn't asked her if anything was wrong, naturally. It wasn't his business, and moreover he hadn't, at the time, wanted to know. He would not have been able to deal with it. He wished now that he had asked.

He wanted to know more about her. He wanted to know what the rest of her mind was thinking about as the sociable bit joked and chatted. He wanted to know what she thought of him. It was important to him to know this, because he wanted her to think well of him.

He did not much like discovering that he wanted this; he didn't see why it should matter to him, except that it was of course her flat and she could always ask him to leave. But it did matter, and he found himself trying to think of ways to please her without making it obvious that he had wanted to please her, because once she knew that about him it opened a terrible hole in his defenses.

His defenses were not in very good shape these days. He had not felt so vulnerable for a long time. He didn't know what to do, because it was clear to him that if he walled himself up again he would lose something he had only just found, which he could not put a name to, which was making everything different, and which he did not think he could again do without.

5

Sergio came to dinner. Rosa and Fabio cooked the meal together: chicken with garlic, accompanied by rice and salad, followed by crème caramel.

"You can do the chicken," said Rosa to Fabio, who had expected to be given bits and pieces to do. And as he stood there uncertainly looking at its plump whiteness, "Well, go on. I've shown you how to do chicken."

So he nerved himself and did it, and although there was no reason why it shouldn't work he still felt astonished and somehow grateful when the first fragrant smells wafted from the oven.

Sergio was not what Fabio had expected. He was tall, for one thing: tall and athletically built, although there was a laziness about his movements. He had an engaging smile, quite boyish, which transformed his otherwise serious face. He was casually dressed and had a rumpled look. He appeared to prefer sitting on the floor to sitting in an armchair. He had an educated voice and a pair of dark-rimmed glasses: these last Fabio had expected. His eyes rested on Rosa with affection.

Fabio watched him.

Sergio had brought a bottle of wine. He opened it, after sorting through the kitchen drawers for a cork-screw with an assurance that annoyed Fabio. He took glasses from a cupboard, poured some wine for Rosa, and brought Fabio a glass in the sitting-room.

Fabio raised it, ironically, but Sergio was already back in the kitchen, doing something officious with the salad dressing.

He seemed not quite certain how to regard Fabio, as though he were puzzled by Fabio's presence in Rosa's flat and Rosa's life and was waiting for the clue to be given that would explain it. He was very polite, however. He enquired about Fabio's job.

"Rosa tells me you're cataloguing a great many arms and legs."

"Among other things," agreed Fabio.

"What other things?"

Fabio described some of the odder features of the collection.

Sergio was interested. "In a way it's a sort of folk-art gallery?"

"Yes, but it's more than that," said Fabio, "be-cause there's a story attached to every exhibit." This had dawned on him one day and he spent much of his working time playing with the idea. "And although a lot of the exhibits look similar, the stories of course would all be different. And in some cases the stories wouldn't really be about what the donor of the exhibit thought they were about."

"A strange idea. What d'you mean?"

"Well, people don't understand the things that happen to them, do they? And they're the center of their own stories, but they're also on the edge of someone else's, and that other story might be much more important, and they don't know what part they're playing in it at all. And people believe lies, don't they? They kid themselves. I think they want to be lied to, really. They need to believe. All the exhibits in that collection have been put there by people who needed to believe. So goodness knows what stories they told *themselves* about what had happened."

Fabio decided he had said far too much and stopped.

Sergio was looking at him thoughtfully. "Do you write?"

"No," said Fabio without hesitation. In the kitchen Rosa directed a glance at him.

"Perhaps you should."

A silence began.

"Could someone give me a hand with the—" called Rosa, and both of them jumped to their feet and collided in the doorway.

"Sorry."

"Sorry."

Over the meal the conversation continued. Sergio wanted to know about Fabio's background, and what his plans were. Fabio's initial gratitude to Rosa for having told Sergio next to nothing about him gave way to dismay, since he did not want to answer most of these questions, did not know how to deflect them and was unable to lie in front of Rosa. He kept hoping that Rosa would rescue him, but for a long time she said nothing. Indeed she seemed to be enjoying the situation.

"What were you doing before you came down here?"

"Oh, various things. My parents expected me to join the family business in Belo Horizonte. It was a bakery and I couldn't stand the thought of it, so I left. I've been traveling around and taking jobs here and there ever since."

"What sort of jobs?"

"Hotels, bars, chauffeuring, working as a guide . . ." He was ashamed of his life.

"You prefer that to settling down somewhere?"

"Yes."

"Mmm. Well, I understand that. Why do the same thing all one's life? Weren't you in Rio before you came here?"

"Yes."

"And what were you doing there?"

Fabio wondered whether there was something about Sergio's job which made him ask questions all the time.

"I . . . oh, I was doing sort of secretarial work for a businessman."

"Lovely city, Rio. Lot of crime there, of course, but a lovely city. I spent a year there once, attached to the University in a rather loose fashion. Some project they didn't want to know the results of when I'd finished it. Did you like Rio?"

"Yes, I did."

"I'm surprised you decided to come down this way,

if Rio was to your taste. Florianópolis is really very boring, you know. It's full of teachers and biologists."

"Speak for yourself," said Rosa.

"Oh—I like it here," said Fabio feebly.

"What line was he in, your businessman?"

"Sergio, have some more chicken," said Rosa. "Fabio cooked it: isn't it delicious?"

"Really? Yes, it's excellent. Just the right amount of garlic."

And the conversation proceeded along safer lines: the best way to cook squid, the sudden unavailability of pimentos, the economic crisis, whether Sergio should buy a new pair of jeans, how much longer the President would last, the municipal elections.

"I suppose Bandeira will get in," sighed Sergio. "Not that it makes much difference, but he is such a blatant ruffian."

"Perhaps it's better to know who you're dealing with," suggested Rosa.

"Perhaps. But I do think it matters when not only are those in office corrupt but they have lost all shame about it."

"Sergio, that's a terribly bourgeois view."

"I'm a terribly bourgeois man."

"What a pity. Do you know," said Rosa, "he came to school the other day, with a retinue of about fifteen, bodyguards and all. Goodness knows whether he expected the fourth form to kidnap him."

"I'm sure the fourth form is quite capable of it."

"You misjudge them. Hearts of gold, every one. He has a handshake like a warm squid."

Sergio laughed. Fabio, who had been frowning over something, said, "What did you say his name was?"

"Bandeira. Roberto Bandeira," said Sergio.

"He's standing for the council?"

"Dear me, where have you been?" said Sergio.

"Do you know something about him?" asked Rosa.

"He's a transvestite," said Fabio.

They stopped eating and stared at him.

"I saw him in Cuiabá," said Fabio, as if that explained it. "He was wearing a green dress and high-heeled shoes."

Rosa pushed her plate away and collapsed into wild mirth.

"Are you sure?" said Sergio. He got up and rummaged in the corner in which Rosa kept old newspapers, and produced a local evening paper which he leafed through. He found what he wanted and laid it in front of Fabio. "That's Bandeira."

Fabio studied the heavy, square face. "Yes, that would be him," he said at last.

"Well," said Sergio, sitting down and reaching for the wine bottle, "perhaps I should have been a psychologist. You don't get excitement like that with plankton."

"Why don't you marry him?" asked Fabio the following evening.

He had not intended to ask this question: it seemed to have been jerked out of him by someone holding a string.

Rosa looked at him in surprise. "I don't want to."

Fabio shrugged. He should mind his own business.

"Oh, all right, that isn't an answer," said Rosa. "It isn't that I'm not fond of him. I think he's the nicest man I ever met. I just don't want to spend my *life* with him." She paused. "What I mean is I don't want to move in with him, cook his meals whether I feel like it or not, and have his children, which is inevitably what I'd end up doing."

"Don't you want children?" asked Fabio.

"No, I don't," said Rosa.

There was a silence. Rosa was used to silences after she made this statement: people could never accept it as a statement about herself, they always took it as a statement about the world, or themselves. Or they didn't believe her.

"I thought all women wanted children," Fabio said.

"You're quite wrong."

He took out a cigarette and played with it.

"Don't you . . . like children?"

Rosa laughed. "Fabio, I *teach* children. Of course I like them; if I didn't I'd be utterly miserable. I like children and I also respect them. I just don't want any of my own."

"Why not?"

He was very persistent. Perhaps, thought Rosa, he had had a painful time with a girl over this very issue; an abortion, perhaps?

"You're assuming," she said gently, "that it's natural for women to want children. Well, if it is there are a lot of unnatural women about. Some mothers don't even like their babies after they've had them: didn't you know that?" (He was wide-eyed.) "Children are a full-time job. I don't want that job. I want the one I've got."

She had lost his attention. He was staring at the floor, still turning the cigarette in his fingers.

"Do you like children?" she asked, but he was far away.

6

Fabio wrote, "Model church, height 29 cm, length 32 cm, white polystyrene decorated with colored sequins; silver foil windows.

"Gramophone, antique, in wooden box with broken lid.

"Tin of needles for above.

"Telephone, antique, earpiece missing.

"Model fishing-boat, length 25 cm, painted wood, with hooked fish on line."

He liked the fishing-boat. It was sturdily made and painted in primary colors, and great care had been taken over carving the scales of the fish, which was as big as the fisherman and bright blue. The story behind the fishing-boat was a children's story; a robust narrative of action, danger and survival.

Some of the stories were sinister. Often Fabio had studied a strange oil painting of two men on a beach. The beach was littered with small cylindrical objects and the two men were picking them up. Cigarettes? Cartridges? But why on a beach? Their faces were ferocious and intent. The brushwork had a tormented quality: it was like the work of a Van Gogh who had everything but the talent. There was a vertical slash in the canvas. The damage might have been accidental, but it looked to Fabio as if someone had stabbed it with a knife.

Some of the stories were not what they seemed. When you began to think about them they became enigmatic. Such was the polystyrene tableau depicting, in the garden of a cottage, a girl dressed in a red cloak, an old apple-cheeked woman sitting at a spinning wheel, and a snarling animal. Red Riding Hood.

What was the point of it? An offering for the healing
of a child whose favorite story this was? Or a com-
memoration of a real event? If the former, the person
who made it hadn't known the story very well, because
Red Riding Hood, grandmother and the wolf should
not all be there at the same time. If the latter, what
had happened? The possibilities were almost limitless.
What, in particular, did the wolf represent?

Unnecessary to speculate on the sailors' caps,
motorcyclists' helmets, builders' hats, riding saddle . . .
lucky escapes, all of them. Occasionally the donor had
literally written the story. Fabio's favorite was the
engine-driver whose brakes had failed. On a large canvas the successive stages of this incident were rendered
in muddy greens and browns. First was shown the loco-
motive, steaming along an embankment: the driver
stood confident on the footplate. Next, a scene almost
identical except that on the driver's face there was now
a look of horror. Immediately afterwards, the engine
was shown plunging out of control down an incline,
while the driver's body was flung doll-like from the
cab. There was a mysterious cloud on the edge of this
picture. Lastly, the engine lay tranquilly on its side in
a field while a bird wheeled above it. The cloud, in the
scene where the driver was pitched from the cab,
proved on examination to contain the Virgin. Lest anything should not be understood, each scene was accompanied by an explanatory sentence in spidery yellow
paint.

Fabio the cynic, the scoffer, the scorner of docility,
worked peacefully in this room. He could not identify
in any way with the mental world of the people who
had made or donated these objects; he regarded them
as a different species. In a detached sort of way he felt
sorry for them, because they couldn't see that they had

been fooled; but he also thought that faith was probably a very comforting thing, so that they had, as it were, got their money's worth. He found it interesting to hear the comments of the few visitors who came up the stairs to inspect the contents of the room, and most interesting of all he found the attitude of Father Luigi, who approved of faith but not necessarily of its products and could not be brought to give an opinon on the subject of miracles at all.

Mrs. Cruz, who talked to Fabio about the collection, her deceased husband and other subjects, was unaware of his ironical thoughts. He felt as if he were in disguise. It was a feeling he seemed to have had for most of his life.

Towards his charges he was tender. His face, as he catalogued the battered antiques, the clumsy paintings, the faded photographs of children long since grown, the dented crash helmets and twisted steering wheels, the fantasies in polystyrene, the watches that had stopped bullets, the little silver figures of angels and saints and the hundreds and hundreds of arms, legs, heads, feet, hearts, livers, thoraxes, breasts and ears in the room's dusty recesses, was attentive and curious. He felt like a custodian as well as a maker of lists, and discussed with Mrs. Cruz whether it might be possible to repair some of the damaged objects in the collection and whether the small admission charge might be increased to cover the cost, or whether on the other hand the exhibits should be left in the state they were in, on the grounds that they had been in that state for so long that it was, as Mrs. Cruz said, "more authentic."

It seemed quite natural to Fabio that he should be doing this job, and once or twice he found himself

wondering what he would do when he came to the end
of it.

Perhaps he could turn some of these stories
into . . . well, into stories. Several of them cried out for
it. He drifted into a reverie sometimes, turning words
around in his head.

7

"You need some fresh air," Rosa said to Fabio. "Come
for a walk."

He was still not going out more than he had to.
Rosa's concern was partly on her own account: she
wanted to encourage him to be more independent. She
hadn't had the flat to herself for weeks. Soon she was
going to have to speak to him again about leaving. It
would be difficult. If he was still holed up like a hermit
crab, it would be impossible.

"I don't need fresh air," said Fabio. He was reading a detective story.

"Yes, you do. Come on."

He put the book down and followed her. Sometimes she wondered if she bossed him around too
much. Could it be good for a weak young man (she
liked him, but he *was* weak) to be living in the flat of
an older woman who kept telling him what to do? On
the other hand, what alternative did she have? He
needed to be told what to do; and even if it was bad
for him he was still, on the whole, in a very much
better state than when he'd arrived. He no longer
walked around as if every step might take him into an
ambush. He was approachable, often he was actually
nice.

It was late afternoon; the heat had gone out of the

day but the streets were still warm and were thronged with people. Rosa and Fabio wandered through the crowds until they came to the square. The red-and-white banner bearing the name of Roberto Bandeira had been joined by several other banners bearing the names of other candidates. They hung like unwound bandages between the graceful trunks of the palm trees, and high above them the green fronds feathered against a blue sky.

Directly toward Rosa and Fabio on his four-wheel trolley, propeling himself with hands gloved in plastic sandals, came a beggar with shriveled sticks of legs. He was surrounded by an escort of whistling, shouting bootblacks. The anarchic little procession reached the center of the square and the beggar, with a practiced flick of the wrist, turned off in the direction of the newspaper kiosk, waving his free hand in farewell.

"I can't understand," mused Fabio, "why it doesn't occur to people that if God cures diseases he must be responsible for causing them in the first place."

"Poverty causes them," said Rosa. "It certainly caused that."

"Well, yes. Working in the church, I've got out of the habit of thinking that way."

"One of the great uses of the Church," remarked Rosa, "is to prevent people from thinking that way."

Fabio grinned. "Do you say that to your pupils?"

"If they're ready for it. You should read the Book of Job."

"The book of what?"

"Job. Old Testament. Poor old Job gets terrible diseases and his children die, and he calls God to account and demands to know why this has happened to him."

"And what does God say?"

"God says that Job's got a cheek asking and wouldn't understand the answer."

"What a system!" laughed Fabio. "It's unbeatable."

"Absolutely," Rosa agreed.

She looked at him as he stood there, head thrown back, face animated.

"You've changed," she said.

He blushed. Glancing round the square, he saw the ice-cream vendors in their invariable place.

"Would you like an ice-cream?"

"Yes please," said Rosa. "Coconut, preferably."

Fabio came back with two ice-creams. They sat on a bench to eat them.

"I love coconut ice-cream," said Rosa. "It must be a year since I had any."

"We should do this more often," he said.

"*You* should. This must be your first outing for a fortnight. I doubt if you talk to a living soul except me and the old dear at the desk from one day to the next, do you?"

"Tell you what," said Fabio."Let's have our shoes shined."

Rosa wanted to say no, but stifled it. Fabio was enjoying himself and a refusal would deflate him. What she felt about the bootboys was guilt, she supposed. And a certain revulsion, which increased the guilt. They were so unchildlike, these children. They knew so much.

Fabio beckoned a boy over and pointed to Rosa's shoes and his own. The boy gave a high whistle and was joined by another. Both knelt, unfastened their boxes and examined the pair of shoes before them with professional care. Fabio's boy began the preliminary brushing almost at once. Rosa's took longer: there was white stitching around the upper which required negotiation.

"How long is it going to take you to catalogue all your gruesome objects?" asked Rosa.

"Another two months, I should think. That's all the time there is, in any case, because the church is going to be renovated and everything is going to be moved out. And obviously they want it catalogued before it's moved."

"*Why* is it being catalogued?"

"Oh, it's an important collection. Mrs. Cruz says it's unique. She says it's the most comprehensive collection of *ex-voto* offerings in the world."

"What does she mean by 'comprehensive'?" wondered Rosa.

"I don't know. But it does seem to contain a model of every organ in the human body," said Fabio. "Plus some that can only be the product of a diseased imagination."

"Is there a model of a diseased imagination as well?" said Rosa, giggling. "Seriously, Fabio, don't you find the atmosphere of the place morbid? I had to get out of there as soon as I walked into it."

"Thanks," said Fabio. "That's why you sent me along there, is it?"

"I thought you had a morbid look about you."

"I just needed a shave."

"So I realized subsequently, but by then it was too late. Well, it doesn't seem to be doing you any harm. It can't possibly be worse for you than what you were doing in Rio."

She was aware, with this remark, of having gone further than she meant to. In fact she still did not know what he had been doing in Rio; they never spoke of it, she assumed he did not want to. She said tentatively, "Are you going to tell me about it?"

He shook his head.

It didn't matter, she realized. She didn't care what he'd done. It was his business.

"You're right," she said. "Don't tell me."

His face, which had tensed, relaxed again and he smiled. Rosa had an impulse to tell him that she was fond of him and was glad he had turned up on her doorstep, but found she was unable to say it. She sensed it would embarrass him too much. Instead, she said, "I'll pay for the shoeshine."

The little bootblacks had finished, and were squatting on their haunches with patient expectation.

"No, I'll pay for it," said Fabio.

They argued amicably over who should pay. Fabio won. He dug in his pocket and brought out a handful of tattered notes. You needed four of them now to pay for a shoeshine: last week it had been three.

Fabio gave the boys a few coins extra. Their dirty faces split with smiles, and they disappeared back into the crowds like fish in water.

"I always feel I should give them some money to buy food," said Rosa.

"They wouldn't buy food, they'd buy *janja*."

The square was quieter now. The light was fading from the sky. In a while people would begin drifting back again, to sit on the benches and meet their friends, to drink beer from cans and listen to the rather bad music provided free each evening by the candidates for the municipal election.

Rosa and Fabio sat on a little longer, before walking back to the flat.

8

The inspector of schools was a small man with thick glasses who moved in a shuffle. He gave the impression of bearing a heavy weight on his stooped shoulders. His head, thrust a little forward as if with anxiety, had a round and tufted appearance. He looked like a capybara.

Rosa felt sorry for him, and forgave him for wanting to interview her in her coffee break.

"Sit down, Miss Van Meurs," he said, indicating a plastic chair with a torn backrest on the other side of the desk. Rosa fetched another chair from the side of the room and sat on it. He watched her without comment and without a smile.

"How long have you taught here?" he asked.

"Six years," said Rosa.

"And before that?"

Rosa gave him the name of the school at which she had first taught. He wrote down her replies in a small, tidy hand.

"Why did you leave that school?"

"I was having to teach a range of subjects, some of which I knew very little about," said Rosa. "Here they wanted a full-time history teacher, and that is my subject."

"Why did you choose history?"

The question startled Rosa. Not knowing quite what he meant by it, she was unable to answer it, but simply looked at him.

He returned her gaze, waiting.

"I . . . It has always interested me," she said at last.

He wrote down this inadequate reply.

"*What* precisely interests you about history, Miss Van Meurs?" he asked in his thin, dry voice that was making her think of a snake.

Rosa was silent as she contemplated her subject: its great unfolding, its mysteries, inexorabilities, cruelties and jests. She did not want to talk about it to him. She did not like this man; and although it was ridiculous to refuse to discuss one's subject with an inspector of schools, she felt he was unworthy of it, in a way in which the least receptive of her pupils was not. She wanted to protect it from him.

"You must know what interests you about it," he said, when after some time had elapsed she had not replied.

"That it is never finished, I suppose," said Rosa. It was as good an answer as any. "That knowledge is always incomplete, and even when we have as much information as we can hope to have about an event we can never be completely sure how to interpret it."

"Interpret?" he said sharply and leaned back in his chair. His eyes ran over her as if to make a new appraisal, the first one having been insufficient. "I'm not sure I understand you. Are you talking about historical theory? Fashions in analysis? You don't subject your pupils to that sort of thing, I hope. They can't have much of a glimmering what you're talking about if you do!"

He gave a short laugh. Rosa boiled.

"No, I mean something simpler than that."

"What do you mean?"

"For instance, since history is usually written by the victors, there is usually an untold story."

"You encourage your pupils to make up untold stories?"

"Sometimes."

"What else do you do?"

"There's the question of context. I try to get them not to approach historical events with hindsight."

"You mean you divorce the events from their consequences?"

"No, I try to make the pupils understand that history simplifies issues which weren't at all simple at the time; that at the time, indeed, it may have been very difficult to see what was happening."

"What is the point of telling them that?"

"It's the truth," said Rosa.

He marked something on his sheet of paper.

"Presumably, if you think history simplifies, you like to divorce events from their causes as well?"

Rosa was not merely furious, she was bewildered. He seemed to be trying to provoke her.

"It's impossible to divorce events from their causes. The job is to identify the causes," she said.

"That has already been done, I would think," said the inspector, "by a long line of historians. But I suppose you disagree with me?"

"I doubt if we can ever identify all the causes of anything," said Rosa. "And even if we did, we would still have to put them in order of importance."

"Dear me, what a doleful prospect. Knowledge is unattainable. Do you teach your pupils that?"

"No, nor do I believe it. I teach them to ask questions."

"Questions? Of whom?"

"History. Themselves. Those who tell them things."

The inspector said nothing for a time. He let the silence draw out, heavy with the words Rosa had just uttered.

"Questions," he repeated at last, as if in the middle

of a serious conversation she had lapsed into some childish vulgarity.

He tidied his papers. "I am obliged to ask you, Miss Van Meurs, what on earth you think you're doing?"

He placed his fingertips along the edge of the desk and lifted his face towards her like a capybara asking for food.

"You talk of interpretation, of the incompleteness of knowledge, of untold stories and 'the question of context'," he said. "I have listened in vain for any mention of historical *fact*. The word appears not to be in your vocabulary."

"I am acquainted with it," said Rosa.

"I'm glad to hear it. At what point, if at all, do you acquaint your pupils with it?"

"They come equipped with it. They know little enough when they come to me, but they are firmly convinced that everything they think they know is in a sacred and immutable category called Fact, and it takes me a long time to shake that conviction."

"Don't try to be clever, please. It won't help you. I am asking you what place you give in your lessons to historical fact. I am speaking of dates, Miss Van Meurs. I am speaking of the names of kings and emperors, and the sites of battles, and the causes and outcomes of wars."

"Oh yes," said Rosa. "I teach all this. Come to one of my classes and question the children. What you call facts, I teach them. But I try to show them that facts rest on evidence, and that evidence can be re-examined."

"And what, I ask again, is the purpose of this toilsome exercise, when you and I both know that in nine hundred and ninety-nine cases out of a thousand the evidence is beyond reasonable dispute?"

"The purpose," said Rosa, "is to turn them into intelligent citizens. And the thousandth case occurs practically every day."

And I have lost my job and I may as well walk out of the room straight away, thought Rosa. She stayed, feeling powerless to move until he released her, and also entertaining a morbid curiosity as to whether the interview could get any worse.

He opened a drawer of the desk and brought out a pile of class books, and she saw that it could.

"I don't think I need to visit one of your lessons," said the inspector.

He opened a book with his thumbnail, as if afraid of dirtying his fingers. He riffled the pages, stained with ink and effort. After a while he read, in his dry voice, the title of an essay: "Write an account of the effects of the goldrush in Minas Gerais in the eighteenth century, including its impact on the Indians." He picked up another book and opened it at random. "Why was slavery thought acceptable in colonial Brazil? Can you think of conditions we now accept which future generations might find shocking?"

He pushed the pile of books aside, and said, "Hypothesis, conjecture, fantasy, interpretation. And *bias*. Through all of this, I detect a consistent and unhealthy bias. Tell me, are you interested in politics?"

"I try to take an informed interest in national affairs."

"Are you a Communist?"

"No."

"No?" In that syllable was such contempt that it frightened her.

"Listen to me," he hissed, leaning forward, not a

capybara at all but entirely a snake, "listen to me, Miss
Van Meurs. Teachers of history are ten a penny, and
out-of-work teachers of history are twenty a penny. We
expect responsibility from our teachers, and that they
will turn out *useful* citizens, not intelligent ones. I
intend to file a very strong criticism of your teaching
methods. You have one month in which to change
them and convince me that you've changed them.
Otherwise—" the little peering eyes behind their pebble glasses were going blind, she thought, and could
have felt sorry for him again in the moment before the
tongue flicked out with its poison—"I must tell you
that your days in the teaching profession are
numbered."

SEVEN

1

"Merciful God, is there nobody in this town who understands how to repair an air-conditioning unit?" demanded Roberto Bandeira, grasping Motta's hand for the briefest moment before delving again into a pocket for a handkerchief with which to wipe his face.

The air in the concourse was still and heavy, and smelt of the cooking in the *lanchonete*. Children whom everyone was too exhausted to stop were kicking around an empty fizzy-drink can. A North American woman complained vociferously about something or other at a desk. Cuiabá airport had not changed.

Motta said, "It's good of you to come at such short notice, Roberto," and steered him towards the exit where the Ford, with its impassive driver, waited.

They drove straight to the mine, not even stopping

to leave their bags at the hotel. Motta talked. Bandeira listened, and his heart sank steadily lower.

"The trouble started a week ago," said Motta. "A delegation of Indians from the reserve turned up at Kurt's office." Kurt was the mine manager. "Kurt said he'd never seen anything like it. They came in full ceremonial dress—feathers, paint, bows and arrows, everything."

Bandeira grunted. He was full of contempt.

"They were very polite," said Motta, "but very definite about what they wanted. They wanted a guarantee that the road over what they are calling 'Indian land' would be closed within two weeks. They said two weeks was plenty of time in which to bulldoze a new road and make temporary bridges."

It was sufficient, thought Bandeira, if they were entitled to ask for it at all. He was struck by the way Motta had spoken of "Indian land" as if it might not be, and for the first time he wondered whether, in fact, it might not be. The Pantanal was not like other land, where fences once put up stayed put up unless interfered with, and rivers kept their course for generations. The Pantanal, subject every year to a flooding without which it could not exist, every year changed its topography. Fences rotted, were broken down by animals, were battered by floating treetrunks or undermined by the relentless water, and were replaced, sometimes years later when almost all trace of them had disappeared, along lines dictated by ideas of where the old fence should have gone, and where it was now physically possible to put the new one. In such circumstances, who could be quite sure where the original boundary of the Indian reserve had been?

He did not say this, yet. He said, "In another two

weeks the rains may have started, and we can't possibly close that road."

"Of course not," said Motta. "In any case, Kurt's instructions are to refuse all requests for its closure short of a direct government order backed up by police."

"So what happened?"

"He refused, naturally. He was polite, the Indians were polite, the Indians went home again and the following night they felled two enormous trees across the road and blocked it."

"*What?*"

In the mirror, Bandeira caught an instantly controlled glimmer of amusement on the black driver's face.

"Yes. Did it with hand axes: quite a feat, really. The logger we got in to shift them said he wouldn't have touched trees like that without his biggest chainsaw and full tackle."

Bandeira could not understand the respect sometimes shown for Indians by educated people who should know better; he put it down to sentimentality.

He said, "If we hadn't come along, they'd still be trying to cut down trees with stone axes."

"Maybe," said Motta. "Anyway, Kurt got the road cleared in three days—"

"It took *three days?*"

"They were *big trees*, Roberto. The side branches had to be lopped before the trunks could be dragged off the road—and you should see the mess the road's in—"

"Savages," said Bandeira, and Motta glanced at him in surprise.

"And you have to remember the difficulty of getting the equipment out from Cuiabá in the first place.

Kurt did a good job. Once he'd got things moving he telephoned me. Unfortunately I couldn't get out here straight away; I must say I thought everything was under control."

He glanced out of the dust-darkened window at the small, impoverished town they were passing through. Soon after this the road turned off into the swampland and the jolting and rattling would begin in earnest. Bandeira, looking at Motta's thoughtful profile, realized that the story, too, was about to take a turn for the worse.

"What happened?" he said again.

"The men were angry," said Motta. "Understandably. Work had been interrupted, they stood to lose their bonus, they were late leaving the site ... And they felt they'd been made fools of."

Bandeira understood that. He felt outraged himself about the road-blocking; but the men who worked daily at the site, lived near it in company-owned trailers and had identified themselves with the mine would have taken the insult far more personally.

"They carried out a punitive raid on the Indian village the night before last," said Motta. "It seems to have got out of hand. Two Indians were killed."

The pitch of the engine fell as the driver throttled back and in a smooth movement pulled the wheel hard to the right. The Ford lurched and rattled as the tires struck compacted earth and rock and sent small stones spinning, striking the underside of the van like pistol shots. Bandeira braced himself against the vehicle's violent motion.

"Two," he said eventually.

"Yes." Motta, who had been talking so fluently, seemed disinclined to say any more.

Roberto thought for a while.

"It was an accident," he said at last.

"Of course it was."

Fixing his eyes on the driving mirror, Bandeira said quietly, "Two Indians are neither here nor there, and we both know it. Hundreds are killed every year in the north."

"True."

"Then what's the fuss about and why have you brought me here? Surely Kurt can square it with the police?"

"The fuss," said Motta, "hasn't yet started. It will start later today, when two anthropologists from the University of São Paulo are due to arrive at the reserve on a fact-finding visit, accompanied by an official from Funai." He gazed out of the window again as if there was something there to be seen, instead of miles of tinder-dry scrub and the occasional bleached carcass. He said softly, "What a pity that wretched woman wrote her letter."

"I've got her on the run," said Bandeira.

"It's too late."

The small stones rapped under their feet. The van slowed, then lurched as the driver prepared to negotiate one of the flimsy wooden bridges across which the road passed at intervals. Bandeira held his breath as they crossed it. They crossed it.

It occurred to him then that there was a piece in the game which had not yet been brought into play.

2

A week after the inspector's visit, Rosa had made no change in her teaching methods.

For the first two days she was in a state of shock.

She did not understand what had happened. It was evident that she had been singled out for unpleasant treatment: the inspector had spent a total of three hours at the school, looking in on various classes and talking to selected teachers, and she was the only person he had interviewed in depth. He had told the headmaster that her work was unsatisfactory and that she must expect a further interview, but had not elaborated.

The headmaster, too, was shocked, but professed helplessness. He said that until specific criticisms were made he could not defend her against them, and that in any case his voice would count for nothing if the Ministry had made up its mind.

Mrs. Souza tried to be comforting. "You're the best history teacher this school's ever had," she said. "Everybody knows it. You mustn't take it too hard, Rosa. We're all behind you."

Rosa thanked her, and tried to repress the thought that it would have been more help if they were beside her. She knew their offers of support were perfectly genuine and of strictly limited extent. She felt bitter about this, but chided herself for it. People could not be expected to risk their jobs for a colleague.

And her job, what of that?

She would lose it, there was no question, and she wouldn't get another one as a teacher. She had no idea what else she could do. It would be the end of everything.

Well, clearly she must give thought to how she could change her teaching methods. What modifications could she make, that would satisfy the inspector?

None, said her heart, terrifying her.

3

Mrs. Cruz liked Fabio. This was apparent from the bright smile she gave him each morning on his arrival, from the way she sugared his coffee to the degree he preferred before placing it before him at eleven o'clock, and from the way she sometimes brought a little cake for him to eat with it. It was apparent from the way she occasionally rested her hand over his for a moment when talking, and from the fact that she talked to him often. There were days when Fabio did less cataloguing than listening.

As a talker, Mrs. Cruz had a distinctive style. She moved her hands a great deal, and gracefully, but she also involved her whole body in what she was saying, for instance throwing herself back in her chair with an expression of amazement when recounting some remarkable event. Her life had witnessed many remarkable events.

She was an observant but kindly woman; some of her anecdotes, in another's mouth, would have turned malicious. But Mrs. Cruz wished to see what was best in people—not out of sentimentality but from an idea that it was not the place or competence of human beings to judge one another. For all she or anyone else knew, mightn't a very small virtue outweigh a very large vice?

Mrs. Cruz also liked to find the best in events. She was an untiring detector of silver linings. She was not a crude practitioner of this art. She did not say, when aircraft crashed and ships sank, that more people would have died if the accident had occurred half an hour earlier. She said that we lived in a world in which fatal accidents were bound to occur, and that we should be thankful there were so few of them. She did not mean thankful to the skill and dedication of certain trained individuals. She meant thankful to the angels who fought day and night to hold the tide of human calamity down to a level at which humans could cope with it.

Mrs. Cruz had a metaphysical view of the world. Everywhere she looked, she saw great forces at work. They shaped the destinies of human beings, but human beings were only one of their concerns. The universe was a very large thing. She surmised that there were parts of it we would not understand. Mrs. Cruz was a Catholic, but not a very orthodox one. Father Luigi was unaware of this. So was Mrs. Cruz.

She was a spiritualist: she believed it was possible to hold converse with the dead. She held regular converse with her husband, who had died twenty-three years previously when leading a dockworkers' strike. In life a rigorous Marxist, he had modified his views since passing over to the other world, and gave her vivid descriptions of his present state. She attempted to convey these to Fabio. There was a lot of light. Music came and went, and flowers featured largely. From time to time there was a rushing wind. Mrs. Cruz seemed to feel there was something inadequate in her account of life beyond the grave, and on one occasion, her eye falling on a pastel-jacketed romantic novel on her desk, she said, "Oh dear, it sounds like one of these, doesn't it?"

"These" were her regular fare. She got through three or four a week. When Fabio asked her why she read them, she said, "Because they all turn out the same way and I don't have to worry about what's going to happen."

She asked him what he read. Poetry, he said for

some reason. A smile of delight lit up her face and she said that her husband had liked poetry, too. Neruda especially, she said. He had taught himself Spanish so that he could read Neruda in the original.

Mrs. Cruz's husband began to interest Fabio. Through the veils wrapped around him by his widow, glimpses of the man could occasionally be caught. He had spent his life in the labor movement, having migrated to the coast from the impoverished countryside of the north-east at the age of twelve, looking for work. Before he taught himself Spanish he had first to teach himself to read and write. He had joined the socialists, but then found himself gravitating in the direction of Communism—"because of the compromises," explained Mrs. Cruz. This was after the Communist Party had been declared illegal. She had met him in São Paulo, when she was a young librarian seeking to broaden her cultural horizons and he was a fire-eating union organizer among the dockers at the port of Santos. He had not been easy to catch: she had pursued him for three years. She had had to read a lot of books about capital and go to a lot of meetings. "Why did you want to marry him?" asked Fabio, perplexed by the gulf between their natures; but Mrs. Cruz just clasped her hands and her eyes shone.

He had remained faithful to the party in its outlaw years, and had gone to prison for distributing subversive literature. That had been a hard time, Mrs. Cruz said; there were three children and only hope to feed them on. Released from prison under an amnesty, he had gone straight back to his political work. Four years later he had been shot by police at a mass rally of striking dockers whom he was attempting, at that moment, to calm.

"I thought, What shall I do?" said Mrs. Cruz.

"There were the children to bring up . . . Oh, it wasn't just the money, that was another thing. The *purpose* had gone out of everything. I thought, I don't want my life. And I couldn't pray: there was nothing there. And then one night, it was about six weeks after he died, he came to my bedside. He made me understand—he didn't speak, you see, he put the words into my mind— that I mustn't grieve, that he'd gone to a better place, and that when I came to join him there I would realize that all our tragedies on this earth were as raindrops in the wind. Yes, that's what he said."

"That's beautiful," said Fabio.

"He always liked poetry. And then he was gone, and I had a wonderful feeling of peace and serenity. It lasted . . . oh, for days."

"But he came back again?" prompted Fabio.

"He came back just as I thought I couldn't go on any longer if he didn't. He said that he would come to see me as often as he was allowed—they can't just do as they like up there, you know—but that I must try to be strong and not depend on his appearances. But then the next time he came, which was the third time, he said that I'd been tested and had passed the test, and from now on he would never leave me. Well, not for long, he meant, because it's about a week between visits."

"You see him every week?"

"Oh yes. He comes on a Thursday night, usually. I don't know why it should be a Thursday, I'm sure."

"And what sort of things do you talk about?" asked Fabio.

"Oh, everything." Mrs. Cruz spread her arms wide and threw herself back in her chair to indicate the universal nature of their discourse. "*Everything*, Mr. da Silva!"

The seriousness of the subject had caused her to break her usual conversational habit. Normally she only called him "Mr. da Silva" when they were discussing the collection; the rest of the time she called him "dear".

4

The days passed, and Rosa did not change her teaching methods.

Regularly she awoke in the small hours convinced that it was the only thing she could possibly do and amazed that even a part of her brain could have thought otherwise. By morning this chill certainty would have dissipated, leaving her again confused, attempting to balance this against that and foresee the future.

She tried talking about it to Sergio.

"You must do what you think best," he said.

This was no help. What *was* best?

It had seemed to her, when the inspector issued his ultimatum, that she was being asked to make a compromise in the grip of which she would rather not continue teaching. To this idea she constantly returned.

As a way of loosening up the problem, however, she tried to consider whether he might be right. *Was* her teaching biased and insufficiently objective? Surely, if it was, so was the teaching of every other history teacher in the country. The accusation of bias particularly incensed Rosa since it was bias—ancient, rooted, invisible bias—she attempted in her lessons to correct. Was the bias *he* wanted—nationalistic and implicitly racist—superior to the bias of which she was certainly guilty—democratic and socialist? This question got no further than its formulation. And did she confuse her pupils, as he had implied? Did she fail them? She looked at their faces, and listened to their questions, and thought she did not.

Then was he asking her to teach what she did not believe?

Not quite. It might have been easier if he had been: the choice would have been clear. He was not asking her to teach that there existed a world-wide Jewish conspiracy or that Germany had not been the aggressor against Russia in 1941. He was asking her to shift her emphasis, that was all. More who-got-what-in-which-treaty. Less discussion.

Surely she could do that?

But what was the purpose of such a shift, where did it tend? It tended towards the fragmentation of knowledge, the learning of facts divorced from their meaning. And this tendency, thoroughly pursued, would result in an uncomprehending view of knowledge and therefore of the world; and the effect of that incomprehension was powerlessness.

Rosa groaned at the intransigence of her conscience.

It occurred to her that her inability to contemplate changing her teaching methods might mask an actual inability to change them. Perhaps she was simply set in her ways, lacking imagination? That would mean she was a bad teacher. Was she? Her colleagues said she was a good teacher.

"Of course you're a good teacher," said Sergio.

"How do you know?" said Rosa fretfully.

"By the way you talk about it."

And there was something else. Time and again she came back to it, although it didn't make sense. It was that there was something arbitrary in the inspector's attack on her. She had an unsettling feeling that it was pointless to try to appease him because it was not a change in her teaching that he wanted, but her head.

Well, it looked as though he would have it.

And how, thought Rosa, will I then survive?

So passed the days. Exhausting though it was, Rosa found cheer in the knowledge that she had not made a decision, that she was still free, still herself. Until it dawned on her that by postponing the decision she was making a decision.

However, that decision-by-default left her still free, and still herself.

In time Rosa saw that this, her feeling of freedom and intactness, was ultimately what was at stake for her. This was disconcerting because she had believed that what was at stake was freedom of thought, the welfare of pupils and the integrity of the teaching profession. Humbled, Rosa wondered if there was any virtue in making a martyr of herself simply because she couldn't live with herself if she didn't; and decided in the end that it was as sensible a reason for martyrdom as any.

An air of unreality had by this time begun to invest the inspector's visit, and there were moments when she wondered if he really could have said the things she remembered him as saying. The only evidence that he had said them was her state of mind, wasn't it? If she could just adopt a new state of mind . . .

Rosa went on teaching as she had always taught, because something inside her cried out at the thought of doing otherwise, and would not be stifled; and because she did not want to see a different look in the eyes of her pupils; and because, in some corner of her mind, she could not believe that anything would happen to her. She was perfectly aware of the absurdity of this. It must be how deeds of extraordinary daring were done, thought Rosa; you simply switched off the brain and kept walking. Heroism was a sort of willed stupidity.

And so things stood the day when Rosa, to her astonishment, opened a letter from Roberto Bandeira asking if he might have the pleasure of taking her to lunch the following Saturday.

5

He was driving a white Mercedes convertible with the hood down. Rosa, looking out of the window, saw it draw up below. Parking was not allowed at that curb, but no one would stop him. He sat tapping his fingers on the wheel, waiting for her.

Rosa had an impulse to drop an egg on him. She resisted it. It would create an interesting scene, but as a result she might never find out why he wanted to take her to lunch.

He became impatient and rang the doorbell as she was on the stairs. When she opened the door he was standing there with a smile of expectation on his face. He took in her appearance in a moment's frank and greedy scrutiny, then gave a little half-bow and said, "Miss Van Meurs, this is a great pleasure."

His transparency aroused her scorn. She was also surprised. Surely that wasn't all he wanted? Surely he could get it easily elsewhere?

He was attentive. He asked her what kind of music she liked, and when she said—mischievously—Mozart, he fished around in a box of cassettes and fed one into the stereo. It wasn't Mozart, it was Tchaikovsky, but at least he had asked. He enquired after her health, her mother's health, the health of her father and siblings. Rosa said they were all well, except her mother who had died eight years ago. He said that his mother's death had left a gap in his life which nothing could fill.

He took the road that wound up into the hills behind the city. He had booked a table at a beach restaurant on the other side of the island, he said; the fish was very good there, he hoped she would like it. Rosa said she was very fond of fish.

He drove like a man who enjoys driving; a big man at the wheel of a big car. Rosa, looking at his wide shoulders and the hand that was several times the size of hers resting on the gear-knob, tried to visualize him in a green dress. It was too difficult. Nothing about him suggested such tastes. She decided Fabio had made an incomprehensible mistake.

They were received at the restaurant with broad smiles and a great show of deference. Behind the deference, Rosa caught curiosity in the waiters' eyes. She flushed a little, angry with them and herself. She shouldn't have come if she wasn't prepared to deal with this.

She looked down the menu. Pricey. The most expensive item consisted of several kinds of shellfish in a sauce and sounded as if it was better avoided. Rosa ordered locally caught fish barbecued with herbs.

Her host raised his whisky glass and clinked it against her *caipirinha*, sending the ice-cubes jigging. "It's not often I have the opportunity of taking a lovely young lady like yourself out to lunch, Rosa. Let us drink to—a better understanding."

"It depends on what you mean by an understanding," said Rosa. She softened it with a smile which felt false. "Why *are* you taking me out to lunch?"

"Both business and pleasure," he said, but seemed surprised to be put on the spot. "Pleasure first. Tell me about yourself."

"I've already told you quite a lot about myself in the car," said Rosa. "Why don't you tell me about yourself? I'm sure it'll be much more interesting."

His reaction amused her: he was irritated at being thwarted, half-aware that she was flattering him in order to avoid doing what he wanted, but fell for the flattery because he couldn't believe that it would *not* interest her to hear about him. He began to talk about himself. He talked—briefly, for he seemed unsure whether or not to be ashamed of it—about his childhood, and then dwelt at some length on the early days of struggle (as he called it) when he was laying the foundations of his fortune. Rosa, rather to her surprise, found that it *was* interesting; but then, he thought he was describing for her the triumphant progress of a self-made man, whereas what she was listening to was the process by which a mind becomes dominated by money and the desire for power, and the techniques it will employ in the pursuit of these, and the stories it will tell itself when it does not like some of the things it has to do. Bandeira even seemed to admit that he had had feelings of doubt about certain deals he had pushed through; here a small family firm driven into bankruptcy; there a man forced to sell property for a fraction of what it was worth; somewhere else a competitor's business falling into his lap because of a rumor fostered . . .

She presumed that by "doubt" he meant moral doubt, but he hadn't said so.

"Do you mean you felt you shouldn't do it?" she

interrupted him to ask at one point, when he was describing a particularly tortuous takeover of a motel chain.

"Oh no," he said. "I didn't feel I *shouldn't* do it. I just wasn't sure I was supposed to do it."

"Supposed to do it? By whom?"

He touched himself lightly on the chest. "My guardian angel."

Rosa laid down her knife and fork.

Reaching inside his jacket, he brought from an inner pocket a transparent plastic envelope containing a faded photograph, and gave it to her. It was of a young woman in a garden, awkwardly posed for the camera and wearing a long old-fashioned dress. She had a sweet, rather anxious smile. The photograph was worn and cracked at the corners: it had been much handled before being placed in its protective cover. Roberto Bandeira took it from Rosa and put it back carefully in his pocket.

"My mother," he said.

"She was pretty," said Rosa.

"She was beautiful."

"And she is your guardian angel?"

"Of course. She lets me know when I mustn't do things."

"How does she let you know?"

"Ah . . ." He gave a little shrug: Rosa shouldn't ask that.

"What sort of things does she say you mustn't do?"

"The last time," said Roberto Bandeira, "was when I was going to fly to Campo Grande for a meeting, and she let me know I shouldn't go. So, although it was an important meeting, I canceled the trip. And do you know, that airplane crashed and twenty people were killed?"

Absorbed in the thought of what might have happened, he took a little lacy handkerchief out of a pocket and wiped his face with it.

After that he must have felt that he had told Rosa enough about himself, because he began to question her about her life, her job and her interests. When he asked her about her job a shadow crossed her face: she felt it and couldn't prevent it, and he saw it. She knew that he saw it by a sudden sharpening of his attention. Something in her was alerted, in its turn, by this and she looked at him carefully, aware how the *caipirinha* and the wine had worked on her to subvert her defenses. It was as if a mask had dropped. He was looking straight at her, straight into her, and she was not a lunchtime companion or a potential mistress, but simply the prey of the predator. It was over in a flash. She stared down at her plate, shaken. There was a skewered fish on it.

"Perhaps you'd rather not talk about your work," he said. "I expect you get enough of it during the week. Tell me something about your father, Rosa. You have an unusual surname. Is he Dutch?"

"My grandfather was," said Rosa. "I never knew him: he died before I was born. My father—" she hesitated. What was there to say? She would have preferred not to say anything.

"You said he was in good health, earlier?"

"He's as strong as a horse, but he's ..." Too late to stop. "He's senile. He's in a nursing home in Blumenau."

"Oh, I'm sorry," said Bandeira. "Do you visit him?"

"Once a month, usually. This month I've left it rather late."

"You've been busy, I suppose."

She was a little surprised. "Yes, as it happens."

"Your work?"

"No, something else I'm involved in."

"Which you aren't going to tell me about?"

"No." She smiled, her placating smile, and wondered why.

"I wonder," said Bandeira, "if I can guess." He pushed his plate away, picked his teeth and said, "Something to to do with a road across an Indian reserve in the Pantanal."

She stared, and her body went cold. A silence seemed to descend on the restaurant, and through it she could hear, for the first time, the crashing of the surf on the beach and the shouts of children.

"You wrote a letter to an American newspaper," said Roberto Bandeira. He refilled her wine glass. She didn't touch it. "Isn't that right?"

Rosa nodded.

"Has it produced the results you hoped for?"

"It's produced a lot of letters for me to answer," said Rosa.

"But it has produced results, hasn't it? Lots of people writing to the paper; there's even going to be a conference, I gather. About these Indians."

"The conference was arranged two years ago," said Rosa, "and it isn't about 'these Indians,' it's to do with the rights of minority indigenous peoples. Which includes Indians among many others."

"Thank you for correcting me. You sound like a schoolteacher."

"I am a schoolteacher."

"But I hear," said Roberto Bandeira, "that you may not be a schoolteacher much longer."

Something in her had waited for this since the moment when she saw him looking strangely at her.

With a sick feeling she said, "You seem to know a lot about me."

"I made it my business to find out."

"Why?"

The waiter chose that moment to remove their plates and ask if they wanted a dessert. Rosa shook her head. She wanted to escape. Bandeira ordered coffee. They waited, not talking, as the waiter brought the two silver pots.

"You want to know why I'm taking such an interest in you?" Bandeira then resumed.

Rosa nodded.

He leered. "Apart from the fact that you are, as I say, a very attractive young woman?"

Rosa, furious, could have thrown the coffee in his face. If she had had the courage.

"Miss Van Meurs—Rosa—I will put my cards on the table," he said. "Your letter to that newspaper has caused me a lot of trouble. I have a business interest in that gold mine in the Pantanal. The road—believe me, your informants have misled you. And I think I'm right in saying that you haven't seen it for yourself?"

"I've seen photographs."

"Photographs! Well, I'll say no more. Perhaps you should have taken the trouble to look at it before you rushed into print with your opinion. It's a very small road, it is doing no harm to anybody, we haven't cut any trees down—although *they* have! Your precious Indians have felled two huge trees, which were probably hundreds of years old, right on the boundary. That's how much they care about the environment! And we need that road, because without it we can't get access to the mine in the rainy season."

"But it isn't the rainy season now," said Rosa.

"Soon it will be." He waved his hand angrily and knocked over the salt.

Seeing him lose his grip on his temper, and understanding at last what this bizarre meeting was about, Rosa began to feel better. She sipped her coffee.

"How has my letter caused you trouble?"

"You've stirred up a hornets' nest. Visits from officials, visits from Funai, letters, telephone calls, inspectors—naturally the men can't get on with their work."

"Well, it wasn't my intention to hinder work at the mine, and I find it difficult to believe that a single letter from me has managed to galvanize Funai into action when it ignores countless violations of Indian rights every year," said Rosa, "but if that's what's happened I can't say I regret it. Heaven knows the Indians have little enough. And what they do have is steadily whittled away by people like you who only care about how much money you can make and don't really believe that Indians should have any rights at all. I know about people like you. You think Indians are animals, don't you?"

She stopped herself. There was a heavy silence.

"I see I can't expect any help from you," said Bandeira.

"Help?"

"I was hoping if I put my case to you, if I explained what we're doing at the mine, all the trouble we're going to to see there's no damage to the environment, using new clean methods of separating the gold, and so on—I hoped you might put in a good word for me with your friends, tell them old Roberto isn't such a bad guy."

Rosa, amazed, studied the pattern on the tablecloth. This is the way it's done, she thought.

She said, "If you're using techniques that don't harm the environment, it's either for commercial reasons or because you have to. But it's irrelevant. You could be running the most ecologically sound enterprise in the whole of Brazil, but you would still have an illegal road going across Indian land."

He said, "How do you know it's Indian land?"

"Of course it's Indian land. It's within the 1968 boundaries of the Indian reserve."

"Is it? How do you know where those boundaries are? Every year the whole region is flooded. The banks crumble, the streams change course. The boundary of that reserve might be anywhere within half a mile or more."

It is difficult sometimes, when your opponent plays his ace, not to feel shocked at what people can resort to. Rosa felt such shock, although she told herself she should have expected something of the kind. At first she could think of nothing to say, because there was nothing that would adequately express her contempt.

Naturally he took advantage of her silence. "I think you're on pretty shaky ground, Rosa," he said.

Rosa found her tongue. "That's the most dishonest fabrication I ever heard," she said. (Well, almost. The Donation of Constantine sprang to mind.)

He shook his head solemnly. "You're on shaky ground."

"If you're so sure you have a strong case, why do you want my help?" said Rosa. "And what influence do you think I have? I'm really not important."

"You had enough influence to get this thing started."

He sounded bitter. He really was upset over what was surely only a minor storm in one of many businesses.

"I have no influence," said Rosa. "It's my father's name. He was one of the country's great experts on Indian culture. Funai has a healthy respect for his reputation."

"I see," said Bandeira. He drank from the little blue-and-white cup. Then he said, "Perhaps there's something I can do for you."

"What could you possibly do for me?"

As soon as the words were out of her mouth, she knew.

"You're going to lose your job," he said.

That was the ace. She felt if she didn't get up and leave this restaurant she would suffocate.

"I have a certain influence," said Bandeira.

There was a silence. Had he expected a response? He went on. "You're an independent young lady, Rosa, and I admire that. But there has to be a limit. At some point you have to accept that you need help. Very well. You need my help. I need yours. How about it?"

"Wait a minute," said Rosa, and her voice sounded strange and thin, like a telephone voice. "You're saying that I'm about to lose my job, but that if I drop my opposition to your road in the Pantanal you'll fix it so I don't?"

"That's about the size of it," said Bandeira. He signaled for the bill.

"What do you know about my job?"

"I hear things."

"What have you heard?"

"Your teaching methods aren't approved of. You've been told to change them or go."

His manner had become brusque. It was the consciousness of power, Rosa supposed.

"And what if I change them?"

He laughed. "You won't. But even if you did . . ." He let the sentence tail off, and shrugged.

Even if she did, it would make no difference. Because she was not required to change her teaching methods. What was required of her was something quite different.

Rosa, remembering her long struggle with herself, and seeing the shabby, shameful little attempt at a bargain which was at the end of it, was nearly blind with rage. She stood up, and as she did so the last piece fell into place for her: that he had been behind the inspector's visit.

"Thank you for my lunch," she said. "You've wasted your time and your money. I don't make deals with crooks."

She walked out, past the openly staring waiters, into the hot glare of an afternoon on the beach.

There was a bus leaving the village for Florianó-polis in half an hour's time. Rosa went into a café and ordered a mineral water, and sat in the shadows by the bar until she saw the Mercedes sweep past. Then she went back to the beach and waded up to her knees in the bright surf.

EIGHT

1

"Tell me about it," encouraged Sergio. Rosa was sitting on the floor of his flat with her back against his legs. He stroked her hair.

"He's a bastard," said Rosa.

"We knew that."

"He tried to flirt with me, he tried to fool me, he tried to bribe me and he tried to frighten me. I think I disliked him most when he was trying to flirt with me."

"What did he want?" asked Sergio, spreading her light, glossy hair that he loved across his knees.

Rosa told him, as briefly as she could while conveying the flavor of Bandeira's approach. Sergio listened in silence.

At the end he said, "What a disgusting man."

"Yes."

"You think he set up the inspector's visit so he would have a lever against you?"

"I'm quite sure he did," said Rosa. "There was something funny about that inspector from the start. Why should he be gunning for me? I don't make enemies. I mean, I don't, do I?"

"No," said Sergio, and then they both fell silent, thinking of the same thing.

"That letter," said Sergio.

"The police found the man who wrote it."

"But why did he write it? He didn't know you."

"I've always felt there was something odd about that as well."

"Would it make you feel better about it, or worse, if you knew Bandeira was behind the letter?"

"Better. It would put all the unpleasantness in one place. And I couldn't feel worse about Bandeira, whatever he did."

"Very rational," approved Sergio. He divided her hair into three parts, three golden rivers flowing down from the hills to the plain. "What are you going to do?"

"Do?" repeated Rosa. "I get anonymous letters and a corrupt inspector. I get bullied and threatened and patronized and leered at, and you ask me what I'm going to *do*? I want a rest!"

"Of course you do. But there's still a decision you can make . . ."

"I've made my decision!" Rosa was indignant.

"I meant—" said Sergio, but Rosa swept on.

"I decided I was not going to change the way I taught to suit some sour little squirt of a fascist inspector who now turns out to be in cahoots with Roberto Bandeira. I decided not to do that, even though not to do it would probably mean losing my job. It cost me a lot to make that decision, but it now appears I could have saved myself the trouble. I don't have to change the way I teach. What I have to do is say I'm in favor of Roberto Bandeira putting a road through an Indian reserve so he can get his wretched gold out. Well I am not going to do that either. They can have my job. They can have anything they damn well want. But they can't have *me!*"

Rosa was on the verge of angry tears. Sergio put his arms round her. "Most certainly they can't," he said.

A little later, he tried again. "What I meant was that you seemed to have resigned yourself to being passive. It might be possible to go on the offensive."

"The offensive!" Rosa laughed. "Sergio! That man owns half of Santa Catarina!"

"So he may," said Sergio. He fetched a bottle of wine and two glasses from the kitchen, and sat on the floor.

"Does it strike you as odd," he said, "that he is so upset over the opposition to this road?"

"Why should it?"

"Because opposition to the siting of roads and factories and so on must happen all the time. He must be used to it. So what's special about this one?"

"It's in the Pantanal. It's difficult terrain. He hasn't got a lot of choice over where he puts a road."

"Granted. But he knew what the Pantanal was like when he went into it."

"Are you saying there's something fishy going on?" asked Rosa. "The company's breaking the law in some way?"

"It's a possibility, and if it's true it gives us a lever against him."

"But how on earth would we find out? Do you know anything about gold-mining?"

"Not a thing."

"Nor do I. Or about the law relating to gold-mining."

"It would seem to be an unpromising tack," said Sergio.

"And if we did find out something, what would we do?"

"Blackmail him," said Sergio blandly. "Two can play at that game."

"Don't be silly," laughed Rosa. "We'd be hopeless at it. Look at us, sitting here drinking wine and playing with the idea of being tough. We're innocents, both of us. What we need is Fabio. He'd tell us what to do."

There was a pause before Sergio said, "He has told us what to do."

Rosa put her glass down slowly.

"Oh, but it's a crazy story," Sergio said. "That he's a transvestite. Don't you think so?"

Rosa said, "When I was having lunch with him he pulled a handkerchief out of his pocket and mopped his face with it. It was a lady's handkerchief."

"Probably belonged to one of his women."

"I don't think so. He would have become conscious of it and put it away, but he didn't. He just wasn't aware that he had anything unusual in his hand. And it was a tiny little lace thing."

"You think it's true, then?"

"I think it probably is. There are more sides to his personality than you'd expect. And Fabio said he'd seen him in Cuiabá, which is exactly where he'd be if he was visiting the Pantanal. It's the nearest place with an airport."

"Then that's it," said Sergio.

"What is?"

"That's the lever."

Another pause.

"Explain," said Rosa.

"Oh, Rosa, it's obvious! Look at who he is, and where he's going. He's got as much money as he wants, so now he's going into politics. He won't stick at a seat on the town council, will he? He's got his eye on bigger things: he may even be thinking of Congress. What's going to happen to that program if it gets out that he likes to dress up in a green frock in the evenings?"

"You don't mean it?"

"I certainly do," said Sergio.

"It's disgusting."

He looked at her sharply. She was sitting with her knees drawn up to her chin, gazing at the far wall. He could not guess what she was thinking, and wondered how often she was, without his knowing it, as far beyond him as this. He moved to touch her shoulder, but she did not respond.

Minutes went by.

It seemed to Rosa that too much had been asked of her for too long. Surely, one hard moral choice should be a person's ration for a lifetime, or at least for a good few years? Yet no sooner had she made one than she was faced with another. She was tired. She wanted to let everything go, let events sort themselves out.

This would not sort itself out. It required an answer. She could feel Sergio's eyes on her, thoughtful, concerned, insisting on an answer.

It might work, she thought. Sergio was quite right: if Bandeira was a transvestite he would do anything to prevent the fact from becoming known. If he was. And if they could . . . Here Rosa's brain became paralyzed as she tried to imagine the process of blackmail itself. What on earth did one say?

And then the decision was made, because she knew she could not do it, whatever it cost her, because to do it would cost her more.

"No," she said, and turned to face him.

"Why?"

"It's a vile thing to do. To blackmail a man because he likes dressing in women's clothes. Because he has a compulsion to dress in women's clothes."

"He is Roberto Bandeira."

"It makes no difference."

"He would stop at nothing to put pressure on you."

"I don't care, Sergio. There are some things that mustn't be done. There are some places you mustn't touch people."

"Even him?"

"Even him."

Sergio made a gesture of defeat. They sat in silence for a time.

2

Fabio wrote, "Diver's helmet, stamped '1931,' picture of Virgin Mary painted inside."

This had been a find. Even Mrs. Cruz had not suspected its existence. It had been at the bottom of a blanket chest full of wooden legs. "Ooh," she'd said, when he unlocked the padlock and eased back the creaking lid, "I wondered where those had got to."

Someone had made an attempt to catalogue the legs. Little gray-white labels, looking like price tags, hung from them on pieces of gray-white string. The writing, spidery and pale brown, was illegible.

The picture of the Virgin, on the other hand, was as bright as if painted yesterday. She was shown ascending, in the usual blue mantle, over the sea. The mantle, the sea and the sky were all the same blue, which made things confusing, but to make clear which was which the artist had outlined the mantle in yellow, put little white wavecaps along the top of the sea, and placed a lurid red sun in the corner of the sky. For good measure, he had added a lurid red moon opposite it. The Virgin's arms were outspread in benediction, but the artist had at this point encountered trouble with the concavity of his surface, and the arms trailed for a long distance as if unable to end themselves, which they did finally in curling fingers which resembled birds' claws.

Fabio would have liked to incorporate some of this visual richness into his catalogue, but Mrs. Cruz said he was to keep the description short. "Once you start *describing* things, Mr. da Silva, well, where do you stop?" she said.

So Fabio set the diver's helmet to one side, affixed to it a sticky label bearing its catalogue number, and applied himself to the wooden legs. There were seventeen of them and they would have to be listed individually. They exhibited a surprising variety. Some of them looked like legs and showed a fair attempt to indicate bone and musculature, and some hardly looked like anything at all, you had to deduce their nature from the context. Wasn't there something odd, Fabio wondered, in using anatomical terms in connection with a model? How could a piece of wood have a femur? And was it quite right to call these things wooden legs since, although that was undeniably what they were, a wooden leg normally was supposed to be something you stood on if you didn't have a real one, which was not what these objects were for at all?

But then, he thought, what *were* they for? What were any of the things in this collection *for*? He had never considered the question. He must ask Mrs. Cruz what she thought about it: it would appeal to her.

"Leg, wooden, (1)," wrote Fabio, absorbed. A shadow fell across his notebook.

In the doorway stood Cesar.

For a moment nothing happened except that the figure of Cesar seemed to grow larger and fill the doorway. Then Cesar moved, quickly as he always did, so that the speed together with his weight and the coldness in his face were shocking. He lunged forward, tore the wooden leg out of Fabio's hand and sent it hurtling across the room into a glass case of pink plaster hearts.

There was a crash, and a silence in which no one breathed.

Mrs. Cruz had risen from her chair and stood with the back of her hand pressed into her mouth. She took her hand away from her mouth and made a sound that was the start of a scream.

Cesar whirled, and clapped one hand over her mouth and the other round the back of her neck.

The door to the tiny room in which they made their coffee was open. Cesar pushed Mrs. Cruz into it and shut the door.

"Keep your trap shut," he said. "Always."

He advanced on Fabio.

Fabio began to back away, but there was nowhere to go. For a moment he tried to shelter, idiotically, behind the fragile bee. He stopped eventually beside the motorbike helmets, from which position he thought he might be able to make a dash for the door.

But Cesar had stopped, too, in a position to intercept him whichever way he ran.

Casually, Cesar began breaking things. He seized

another wooden leg and smashed the glass in the nearest cases with it. He pulled things out of the cases with one hand, still swinging the leg in his other hand, and threw them across the room. Statuettes, framed photographs and a clock crashed against the wall. The clock fell on another case and broke it.

All the time his eyes scarcely moved from Fabio's face.

Cesar threw half a dozen steering wheels, spinning like quoits, and then the saddle. The last missed Fabio narrowly and brought down a shelf of surgical appliances.

Fabio could not move. The most frightening thing about what was happening was that Cesar did not appear to be angry. He was methodical, almost impersonal.

Cesar lifted the polystyrene garden of Red Riding Hood, dropped it to the floor and put his foot through it. He took the flimsy tin airplane in his hand and broke the wings off it.

"You're coming with me," said Cesar.

Fabio shook his head.

With his left hand Cesar picked up the wooden fishing-boat and dropped it on the floor. Fabio watched as he lowered his heel on to it.

"You'll come with me," said Cesar, "because you know that I'll kill you if you don't."

Fabio did know it.

3

The 9:35 a.m. bus from Florianópolis arrived at Blumenau approximately three hours later, depending on the driver's mood. This was the bus which Rosa normally caught when she visited her father. She would eat a hasty snack at the bus terminal before catching another bus into the city center, after which she would have to take a third bus to the suburb in which the nursing home was situated. It would have been pleasanter—and it would have occupied part of the time— to have lunch with her father, but he would not let her. Several times, during his first year at the home, she had written to say that she would take him out to lunch, only to discover, on arrival, that he had had lunch in the dining-room. He said he got hungry and couldn't wait until the middle of the afternoon (it was 1:45), and why couldn't she get there earlier (although she had told him there wasn't an earlier bus). Once Rosa took him to an expensive German-owned coffee shop for coffee and cakes instead. He said the coffee (which was excellent) tasted burnt, and poked with his fork at the exquisite cream-filled pastry that was going to cost the remainder of Rosa's weekly budget.

Rosa interpreted this behavior as a desire to upset her. He had acted on this desire for as long as she could remember and she saw no reason why he should stop now. However, in time she realized that she was not being quite fair. He liked the food at the nursing home—dull, plentiful, featuring bratwurst on Wednesdays—and he hated changes in his routine. These factors had to be added to his desire to upset her.

His mind was decaying. She had to keep reminding herself of this, because he looked so healthy and because the childishness, irresponsibility and unkindness he demonstrated on her visits were the childishness, irresponsibility and unkindness he had demonstrated all her life. He was still perfectly rational if you analyzed his thought processes. It was their starting-point that was often illogical or arbitrary and threw the listener into confusion. And he forgot things. He forgot who she was, every time.

When he needed to remember something in order to score a point in argument, his memory was perfect.

If Rosa had not had the assurance of several doctors that her father was suffering from a clinical disease, she would have believed that he was laughing at all of them and enjoying the most untrammeled power he had ever exercised. There were times when she did believe it.

She was the only member of the family who visited him regularly. Her younger brother, Artur, went to see him whenever he had long enough leave from his ship. Hugo, managing a petrochemical works in Recife, did not visit him. He had never forgiven his father's description of the girl he intended to marry as a squint-eyed gold-digger.

Rosa calculated, as she sat on the bus that went to the nursing home, that this was her fifty-seventh visit. Fifty-seven of these journeys on which she couldn't even read because on the way there she was too tense and on the way back she was too exhausted. Why did she do it? He didn't care whether she visited him or not. At least, he appeared not to. He never said, "Thank you," or that it was nice to see her, and often he seemed irritated by her presence. Yet he would say, "Next time you come," and give her instructions as to what she was to bring, which he would have forgotten requesting and would not want when she brought it.

This time she had brought him an almond cake and some chocolate. He would reject them both, but would have taken possession of them by the time she left.

He was standing with his back to her as she walked up the drive, talking to one of the nurses. The nurse saw and greeted her, and said, "Here's your daughter, Dr. Van Meurs."

He turned. As always, there was a moment when Rosa was five again and frightened. He was so tall; still, now, he seemed to tower over her. He was wearing shorts and an open-necked shirt, and his limbs were firm with muscle and suntanned. His eyes looked very blue. In his crinkly fair hair there was hardly any gray.

He looked at Rosa and said, "That's not my daughter."

"Yes, it is," said the nurse. "It's your daughter Rosa."

"My daughter doesn't visit me."

"Oh, what a fib," said the nurse. "Only this morning you were telling me that she visits you every month and that she would probably be here today."

"Hello, father," said Rosa, and kissed him on the cheek.

"Have a lovely afternoon," said the nurse, and went away.

"What's in that box?" he said.

"It's an almond cake," said Rosa.

"Is it for me?"

"Yes."

"I don't like cake," he said.

"Oh dear, what a pity," said Rosa. "Well, I can always take it home again. Fabio's very fond of almond cake."

"Who's Fabio?" he asked sharply.

"Your nephew," said Rosa. "Shall I tell you about him?"

"I haven't got a nephew," he said. "Why have you come back here? I don't want to see any more bits of paper."

"Let's sit down, shall we?" said Rosa.

They sat in deck-chairs in the shade of the trees. The lawn sprinklers had been switched on and from time to time the breeze blew a gust of spray in their faces. Rosa found this disconcerting; her father seemed to enjoy it.

Conversation was always difficult at first, until he had accepted her presence sufficiently to start talking; and he would then resent her contribution, which made it less a conversation than a monologue. Often she found it difficult to understand what he was talking about, when he did start to talk. This was because what he said had no context: he never explained anything. Sometimes she thought he was becoming paranoid. But then, hadn't he always been?

She began to tell him about Fabio's arrival. Fabio, in fact, had not come home the previous night, but Rosa had no reason to think that his absence was more than temporary. At the back of her mind was the idea that her father would accept Fabio as the reason for the lateness of her visit this month.

"Fabio is Hendrik's son," she said.

"Hendrik?"

"Your brother."

"I haven't—" he began, and stopped, presumably bored with it. He said, "How d'you know he's Hendrik's son?"

"Why on earth should he pretend to be Hendrik's son if he isn't?" laughed Rosa.

"People pretend to be all sorts of things," her father said.

"Well, he really is Hendrik's son. He looks a bit like you, actually."

Her father smiled. Then, "Where's Artur?" he asked.

"He's on a boat somewhere."

"What the devil is he doing on a boat?"

"He's in the navy, father."

"Oh yes. Stupid thing to do. I suppose I wasn't good enough for him."

"I think he felt he wasn't good enough for you."

"Oh no, he didn't. He never felt that," said her father. He leant back in his chair and closed his eyes.

"Fabio is working in a museum," said Rosa.

He opened his eyes. "What museum?"

"A religious museum. Attached to a church."

"Oh, a church," he said dismissively. Religion was the only subject on which Rosa and her father had ever agreed. "Perhaps those men were from a museum," he said, "though they didn't look like it. But then, how should I know? I never go anywhere. I haven't been to a museum for years."

"Would you like to go to one now?" said Rosa, suddenly alert. She glanced at her watch: there was time. What a good idea. Why had she never thought of it?

"No," he said.

Rosa settled herself again in her chair. In a while she could go and get him an ice-cream, and that would occupy ten minutes. They could walk around the grounds. Someone might come up and talk to them. A tree might fall.

"Fabio—" she began.

"Oh, for heaven's sake stop twittering about Fabio. I've no idea who he is. Can't you talk about something interesting?"

Rosa took a deep breath. "I might lose my job. Is that interesting?"

He was roused to attention. "Why?"

"An inspector visited the school and interviewed me. He doesn't like the way I teach."

"What's wrong with the way you teach?"

(Was it imagination, or was there belligerence in his tone, and on her behalf?)

"Not sufficiently fact-oriented," said Rosa. "He wants more names of kings."

"*Kings*," said her father with profound contempt. "Diet, that's what historians ought to teach."

"Diet?"

"What people ate. Far more important than who their kings were."

"I'm sure you're right."

"Diet, sexual practices, attitudes to child-rearing. Study of Indian culture should be compulsory in schools."

"Fat chance of that," said Rosa. "As a matter of fact—"

"The Guiacurú, now, had some interesting attitudes."

Rosa hunted for the Guiacurú, and found them. At least, she thought she had.

"The horse-riding tribe of the plains?"

"Lived and died on horseback. They broke their horses in the rivers, you know, so they'd have less far to fall."

"How intelligent."

"Indians are highly intelligent. I thought you knew that. They had a slave tribe, the Guaná, who used to come and till the fields for them and serve them in their tents. But it wasn't slavery as we would understand it, because no orders were given, and no coercion was used, and the Guaná would go home whenever they felt like it."

"So it was voluntary?" said Rosa.

"It was the way it was. And the Guiacurú would share with their Guaná workers what they had. Their wives, sometimes."

"But there was no payment?"

"No."

"What would have happened if one year the Guaná didn't come to till the fields?"

"It would have been inconceivable."

Rosa thought about it. "It's a subtle relationship," she said.

"Of course it is. Too subtle for us."

"Is that what you meant by interesting attitudes?"

"They had transvestites, too."

Rosa sat up. "Male transvestites?"

"Yes, of course. What would be the point of female ones? They performed sexual services for the warriors on campaign. Too dangerous for women to go, you see."

"Rubbish, they wanted to keep all the excitement to themselves. It's always the same," said Rosa.

Her father ignored this. "The transvestites did women's work as well. They spoke in high voices. They even pretended to menstruate."

Rosa was baffled.

"It drove the Jesuits crackers," said her father with satisfaction, and fell asleep.

After a few minutes he woke up and said, "There's a monograph, if you're interested. It's by . . . Damn. Frenchman. You know who I mean."

"I'm afraid I don't," said Rosa.

He tapped the sides of his chair. "Damn. Now, how could I forget that?"

"It'll come to you," said Rosa.

"Yes, it will. It'll come to me in a minute."

They sat for a while and watched the birds squabbling over something in the grass. Then Rosa said, "Somebody's put a road through a Bororo reserve in the Mato Grosso."

"I don't want to hear any more about it," her father said.

"This is the first time I've mentioned it, father."

"Those men were talking about it all afternoon. I thought they'd never go."

"What men?" asked Rosa, whose feeling of pleasure after the conversation about the Guiacurú had abruptly vanished.

"They came to see me with briefcases. They didn't look like people from a museum to me."

"When was this? What did they want?"

"I don't remember. Yesterday. Oh, I don't know. They were here for a long time, talking away. Soil erosion or some such thing, I don't know. What do I know about soil erosion? I'm an anthropologist, not a geographer. I didn't understand it. Anyway, they had a letter they wanted me to sign and I signed it, and they went away. I expect they'd still be here if I hadn't."

"You signed something?"

"Yes, I told you."

"What did it say?"

"Something to do with soil erosion and boundaries. You never listen, Rosa."

"Who was the letter addressed to?"

"Oh, to Funai. Lot of idiots. It was to help the Bororo. It won't, of course."

"But who were these men?" persisted Rosa.

"I don't *know*," said her father. He was becoming agitated. "You shouldn't ask me all these questions. I can't cope with it. That's why I'm here."

"I'm sorry," said Rosa, "but it's really important for me to know who they were."

"I don't know who any of these people are," said her father. "I don't know who you are, half the time."

4

During the flight to Rio, Fabio hardly spoke. Cesar sat beside him, his bulk filling out his expensive, flashy gangster's suit. Fabio could feel the warmth of Cesar's body through the suit. It nauseated him.

He closed his eyes and tried to escape into his thoughts, but there was nowhere to go. He could think of nothing but the oppressive bulk in the seat next to him. He tried to formulate ways of getting away from Cesar—could he make a dash through the baggage hall, or jump out of the taxi?—but again his imagination stalled. He was unable to visualize these acts because he knew they led nowhere. There was nowhere to go.

Perhaps one day, he thought, somebody would kill Cesar, and that would free him.

He spoke once without being compelled to. "Why do you want me back?" he asked.

"Business is expanding," said Cesar. "You've got the touch."

Fabio looked out of the little window. They were flying up the coast: below them a green, white-capped sea; on their left the coastal cities and, behind those, the tawny hills. Ships steamed, highways snaked, houses clustered, all, from this height, orderly, and in their smallness touching. Down there people, invisible, went about their lives. Some of them knew Cesar.

Cesar said they were going back to his flat, and the following day would go to the farm. He wanted

Fabio to stay there for a while. Mario had hurt his leg, and Ana needed "help around the place."

Not the farm, thought Fabio. Not the farm, with its gloom, its evil smell and its misery. But it was shrewd of Cesar to take him there. It was miles from a proper road, and even that road carried little traffic. It would be easy enough to escape from the place, but he would still be walking when they picked him up hours later.

And where was there to go?

The taxi at the airport took them straight to Cesar's flat. Fabio spent the afternoon and evening there, performing a miscellany of jobs which Cesar found for him and which might, if he had been sufficiently curious, have informed him further about Cesar's diverse interests; but he was not curious. He found himself at one point counting polythene sachets of something or other, at another point filling boxes with books in sealed wrappers, at another addressing envelopes, but felt too deadened to care what was in the one or to whom he was addressing the other. He slept on a camp bed in a room full of the cardboard boxes he had filled with books.

In the morning they drove to the farm. Cesar drove, erratically as always, expecting the car to take care of itself.

The air of decay was stronger than he remembered. The place looked derelict in the brilliant noon light. A thin black dog, Mario's gun dog, ran out to greet them. Just inside the gate was the stinking, fly-covered carcass of some small animal. The dog nosed it briefly before turning to follow them.

Ana, stone-faced, was washing clothes in the trough in the yard. In the kitchen Mario sat with one leg stiffly in front of him resting on a chair. He was cleaning his rifle. He nodded respectfully to Cesar, and stared at Fabio.

"Any trouble?" Cesar asked.

"Nothing she can't handle," chuckled Mario.

"Well, let's take a look," said Cesar. He took a key from his pocket, then, seeming to change his mind, tossed it to Fabio.

"Go and check on the property," he said. "You'll be keeping an eye on it for the next few days."

Fabio walked down the flagged passageway. It would not be so bad. He had seen it many times.

He opened the door.

She was about two and a half. She sat on the floor in a tangle of dirty bedclothes, clutching a toy. She looked at him, eyes dilated with fright, waiting to see what he would do.

NINE

1

When Fabio did not come home on the Friday night, Rosa was surprised but not perturbed. She told herself that he had at last done something normal and got himself a girlfriend. When he didn't come home on the Saturday night she wondered if he was all right, but did not think about it for long because, having just returned from visiting her father, she had a great deal else to think about.

He didn't come home on the Sunday night, either.

Rosa, ignoring the voice of alarm at the back of her mind, told herself that it was not her business where Fabio was. Nor did it mean anything that he had not got in touch with her. How could he? She had been out for most of the weekend. And hadn't she wanted the flat to herself?

On Monday morning she left him a note. It was

terse with suppressed concern. It was still there when she got home from school in the afternoon.

Rosa stood looking at it. Sun beat through the windows of the flat and made patterns on the floor. Flies buzzed. There was sugar on the draining-board where she'd made the coffee in a hurry.

The voice at the back of her mind screamed at her that something was wrong.

Rosa left the flat and walked quickly through the streets that led to the church. She went in at the side entrance, along the cool passage, and stopped. The green door at the top of the stairs was shut, and there was a notice pinned to it which, even at this distance, she could read: *"Closed indefinitely."*

There was no point in going up the steps, trying the door, knocking, and peering at the notice as if it contained a hidden message, but she did all these things. Then she stood at the top of the steps, with a feeling of dread growing inside her, trying to tell herself that nothing out of the ordinary was happening.

Someone must know something. She clattered down the steps—noise is reassuring—and entered the church. Its stillness arrested her. A solitary worshipper knelt among the seats. Candles cast an upward glow over the mellow golden paintings.

Rosa walked down the side aisle, past the watching saints. She sat down on a rush-bottomed seat which was joined to fifteen other rush-bottomed seats—as if it were a sort of airplane, she thought—and allowed herself to sink into the silence, hoping that in it there might be something she could use.

There was nothing. After a while she got up and left.

Back in her flat, she drank a lot of coffee and tried to think it out. Fabio's absence *was* abnormal. The premature closing of the museum *was* strange. Were they connected? It was an unlikely coincidence. If they were connected it seemed to make Fabio's absence more worrying, because if he had left because his job had finished he would certainly have said goodbye to her.

She had not wanted to ring the police, but she now realized that to delay doing so any longer was stupid, and rang them from Marcia's flat. No information had come in about an accident to anyone of Fabio's description.

After a further half-hour's worried indecision Rosa concluded that she must go back to the church, find the priest or caretaker and discover how long the museum had been closed. That would be something concrete.

When she returned to the church it was shut, and persistent ringing on a bell set into the wall at the side elicited no reply.

2

Fabio positioned the log and rested for a moment with his hands on the axe handle, sizing it up. Some of these logs were so big that a blow in the center merely trapped the blade; you had to find the line down which they would split.

He found it, shifted his feet wide apart and swung the axe, relishing as always the moment when, sliding his hand up the smooth haft, he relinquished control of its downward momentum to the weight of the axe-head, which hurtled into the brittle wood. The pieces flew from the blade.

Fabio grunted with satisfaction. He repositioned the larger piece for another blow of the axe.

He swung, and smote. The wood flew, cleanly halved.

Fabio wiped his face with his forearm. He was streaming with sweat. He straightened up, with groaning muscles, and glanced at the sun. It was almost overhead. The midday meal would be ready.

He began to throw the split logs into the back of the pick-up. But when he had finished he did not immediately climb into the driver's seat and start down the track to the farm. He sat for a while on a tree-trunk, looking into the valley. From this vantage point the farm was not visible, being tucked behind a fold of the hills. That was one reason why he liked it up here, and had in the past few days split enough wood to last the farm for a month—or so at least Mario said. Fabio had pointed out that there was no knowing how long Mario's leg would incapacitate him.

Even so, he would have to find something else to get him out of the house tomorrow. There was the livestock: a few scrawny hens, some pigs and four goats. One of the goats gave milk; there was no point to the others that Fabio could see. The pigs, of which he had not ascertained the number, wandered about and were often to be found in the house. The house was filthy. There was no order or purpose in any of it. Ana worked ceaselessly, her face set in a mask of bitterness, without making any visible impression on the squalor around her. Mario, if the tasks outlined to Fabio were any guide, appeared to do very little except chop wood, shoot rabbits and make sure the pigs were shut in at night. Fabio was ignorant of farming, but he knew this wasn't a real farm.

He must get back: Ana hated it if he was late. She cooked meals in which the meat, if any, was like leather and the rice was lukewarm and came in gluey lumps. Fabio thought of Rosa, and Rosa's casual, inspired cooking, and pushed the thought out of his mind.

He got into the pick-up, in which the driver's seat was broken, the suspension appeared to be on the point of disintegration, and in which it was pointless contemplating a getaway because there was never more than a couple of liters of petrol in it, the key to the petrol store being in Mario's pocket. Fabio drove, with necessary care, down the rutted track.

"We've been waiting ten minutes," Ana greeted him.

The child sat in the high chair that was kept for them. She looked at him as he came in, then back at the mess of mashed black beans and rice Ana had put in front of her.

"Don't chop any more wood, we've got enough," Mario said.

Fabio grunted, and helped himself to beans.

The child's spoon was poised over the food. She was staring round the room.

"Does she eat?" asked Fabio.

"Of course she eats," said Ana angrily.

Fabio took a forkful of beans. Too much salt. He dug hastily into the rice, which had congealed. The combined effect was horrible. Without meaning to, he pulled a face. He looked up, then, and saw that the child was watching him. For her benefit he exaggerated the grimace. It was a way of saying he didn't like the food any more than she did.

On her face appeared the faint glimmer of a smile.

Delighted, Fabio grinned at her. The smile started to grow.

Ana got up, took a spoonful of bean mush and poked it into the child's mouth. She began to cry.

Fabio forced himself to look at his plate, and go on looking at it, and look at nothing else.

He had never been able to cope with this. The document-faking and the ritual dance with officialdom and the clients had been a sort of game, and much of the time he had been able to tell himself that they *were* the job, but when he came face to face with the miserable children on whom the whole commerce was based he had always experienced a moment of panic. He retreated from it into callousness. Callousness blunted his feelings and stifled his thoughts, and put a barrier that should have been impassable between himself and the children he was handling. But callousness didn't always work. It had cracks in it. Feelings he didn't know he had, didn't know he was capable of, would visit him in the night. Horror, pity. He fought them back to their caves, but he could not extinguish them. And the children . . . God, didn't they *know*? They had been stolen from their families, dragged across the country, roughly treated and left to the dreadful mercies of Ana. Yet when he went to collect them they looked at him with—of all things—hope. They tried to talk to him. They thought he was taking them home.

Those endless journeys, as he tried to block their half-articulated, crystal-clear questions. As he handed them over, they would clutch at him. After three hours' acquaintance, he represented safety. He would smile, a smile that he felt must look like a mask, and walk away.

It was no better if they were too young to talk. They would look at him instead.

He told himself there was no reason to believe they would come to any harm. Indeed, the high price that was paid for them, particularly the fair-skinned ones, was presumably an indication that they were going to homes where children were desperately wanted. But sometimes he knew they were not going to a home, that he was handing them over to an agent. And in any case he had spent enough time with nervous clients, tampered with enough documents that had something funny about them in the first place, detected often enough a whiff of fear when fear should have been out of place, to know how often people didn't want children for the reasons they said they did.

In the end the weight of his revulsion had propelled him down an escape route as soon as one opened. And now he was back, as deep in it as ever, and less able than before to protect himself because he had stupidly allowed himself to get softened up in the interval.

So unable was he to cope properly with the situation that he couldn't even conceal his feelings from Ana and Mario.

Not, he supposed, that there was any reason why he should. They had never liked him, and if now they thought he wasn't to be trusted what difference did it make? He had no wish to be here; it didn't matter whether they trusted him or not. Except that if they didn't it would make it impossible for him to . . .

What?

He lowered his fork and stopped eating, astonished at the idea that had flitted through his mind. If they didn't trust him, it would make it impossible for him to help the child.

In his wildest dreams, it had never occurred to Fabio that he might *help* any of these children. Of course it was exactly the opposite of what he was being paid to do, but surely one reason why he had never thought of it was its total impracticability? How could they be helped, except in unimportant ways by little acts of kindness that might even, by raising their expectations, make their predicament worse? They had been torn out of their world. They were lost. The only way to help them was to return them to their parents, and no one, no one on earth except these frightened and inarticulate children, knew who their parents were.

He looked at the child in the high chair. Her face was grimy, swollen from tears and smeared with food. Under the mess, she was fair-complexioned with pale blond hair. She would be a valuable one. Her name was Liza, but no one called her by it: names were not encouraged in this house. He wondered where she came from. Some of these children came from the other side of Brazil. One or two he'd dealt with hadn't come from Brazil at all. This girl might have come from anywhere.

She would hold the memory of where she came from for a little longer, and then she would forget.

It was ridiculous to think that he could help her. She must wait here, like all of them, for her buyer.

Mario said the pigsty needed cleaning out.

The bedding, which resembled black seaweed, oozed underfoot. Fabio's stomach rose at it. He forked the stuff out through the door and carted it, in foul steaming lumps, to the field where Mario said he was to scatter it. Similar lumps had been spread there before, and showed as bleached-out mounds through which a few blades of grass grew. Between the mounds the soil was parched. Fabio spread his glutinous load, got buckets of water from the pump and sluiced the floor, then fetched fresh straw from a barn. After that, wanting to be both clean and as far as possible from the house, he walked half a mile to where the stream

fell into a wide pool between rocks, and bathed. Being
fairly shallow, the water was warm. Fabio washed his
clothes and spread them on the rocks to dry. He
stretched out on the bank in the sun and smoked a
luxurious cigarette.

Cesar was in the kitchen, shouting, when he
returned.

"Clean this damn place up, for Christ's sake. What
d'you think I pay you for?" (The filth on the floor, the
cobwebs with their ancient burdens, the bloodstains
on the wooden table.) "What's the client going to think
when I bring him here? He's an important man. And
that girl's worth a lot of money. We're running a high-
class operation here. You get this place looking clean
by Sunday or you're out on your necks, both of you."

He rounded on Fabio. "Where the hell have you
been?"

"Cleaning the pigsty," said Fabio.

"This whole damn place is a pigsty," said Cesar.

He left, the car's exhaust roaring in the walled
yard.

"I'm taking Liza out," Fabio announced the next
morning.

"Out?" Ana appeared not to have heard of the
idea.

"Yes, to get some air. Look how pale she is."

"She isn't allowed out," said Ana.

"Why not?"

"Orders."

Fabio picked up the child and walked off with her.
She squirmed in his arm: it was a strange feeling, not
unpleasant.

"It's all right," he said. After a while she stopped
wriggling and settled down, riding easily on his hip.

He walked quite fast until they were out of sight of the farm, half afraid that Mario would send the dog after them, but nothing happened. The earth was warm and a haze rose from it. A brilliant-colored bird flew across their path: he couldn't identify it, he didn't know birds.

"Bird," she said clearly.

He was so surprised that he stopped and looked at her. She looked back at him, candid, questioning, a bit surprised at his surprise.

"Yes," he said, "that was a bird."

She nodded.

Fabio walked on. He was suddenly aware of the danger of what he was doing, of its irreversibility. He could still take her back. He didn't.

Further on he realized that it was all right to put her down. She might like to walk. He set her carefully on the ground, and she took his hand and began to trot beside him. The "trot" was a sort of bouncing half-run that contained a suggestion of pent-up energy, as if the child were a spring. She probably hadn't been out of doors for the past week. He tried to imagine what a week was like when you were two and a half years old.

She began to sing. A tuneless, wordless lilting song that rose and fell and meandered like a stream. The song turned into an exuberant shout as a butterfly passed them.

"Buff—"

"Butterfly."

"Butter fly."

When they reached the pool she gave a shriek of delight and ran towards it. "Careful!" yelled Fabio and lunged after her. She danced away.

"Okay, just don't fall in," said Fabio, "because I'll have a lot of explaining to do."

Liza began clambering over a tree root to get to the water's edge. Fabio, alert to fish her out the moment she slipped, sat on the bank and watched.

She didn't slip. There was a natural wariness in her actions that was like an animal's. She progressed in an organized way over the tree root, reached the water's edge and stood there, singing her lilting song.

"Come and take your shoes off," called Fabio.

She laughed as if he had made a huge joke. Her sandals were already soaked. Ana would be furious.

A wave of rage at Ana passed through his whole body, leaving him breathless. Recovering, he went down to the water, where he knelt in the damp sand around the tree root and took off her sandals. Her feet were strong-looking and chubby: a child's feet, flat along the sole. Tiny, determined toes. They dug into the sand with interest. Then she raised one foot and brought it down with a smack on the water, splashing him, and laughed.

She was obviously going to get as wet as possible. He undressed her, and held her hand while she waded into the water up to her knees, splashing and shouting. She loved it. Was it safe to let her go? Or should he get in too? He hadn't intended to, but he found himself taking off his jeans and shirt and slipping into the pool. Liza hurled herself at him. They played. They splashed each other with water. Fabio tried to teach her to swim. She didn't really get the idea.

When, eventually, he thought she'd had enough, he hauled her out, dried her with his shirt and said, "What shall we do now?"

"Go in water," she said.

"Well you can't. You've done that."

"Yes. Go in water."

"I'll tell you what," said Fabio. "We'll make boats."

He made a series of boats out of what lay around— scraps of paper, leaves, tree bark. Some were quite elaborate. The leaf boats were just leaves. Some of them weren't much good but all of them, in the end, did the magical thing that was required of them: they described a circle round the pool, were caught by the current and floated through the narrow gap between the stones to join the stream, where they bobbed about gratifyingly for a time before disappearing from sight or getting lodged in the bank.

Liza watched each one intently. Sometimes she held out her hand for the boat so she could put it in the water. When at last Fabio stopped and sat back on his heels, yawning in the sun, she ran and brought more leaves and pressed them into his hand, and he began again, obediently.

The client was from the USA, as Fabio might have guessed from Cesar's manner. Cesar admired Americans.

Mr. Stead was middle-aged and paunchy, with deep shadows under his eyes and square rimless glasses. He wore a business suit and gleaming black shoes, in which he picked his way fastidiously through the house.

He took in at a contemptuous glance the mean fur- nishings of the room Cesar called "the nursery," and then his gaze alighted on Liza, who was sleeping after her meal. His face changed. It did not soften, rather it expressed a sort of alert satisfaction, as if he had found something he had been looking for.

"She is prettier than her photograph," he said. His Portuguese was perfect.

Liza woke up. She looked at the faces around her

and seemed to be on the point of crying. Ana moved forward and picked her up, and then she did cry, and held her arms out to Fabio. After a moment's hesitation he took her.

There was a surprised silence. Ana looked furious.

Mr. Stead was unaware that anything had happened. "What did you say her name was?" he asked. "Liza?"

"That's right," said Cesar.

"Well, Liza, would you like me to be your new daddy?"

She shrank into Fabio's shoulder.

"Well, well," said Mr. Stead. "She'll soon get used to me. It takes them a little time to settle down."

"Of course it does," said Cesar. "It's natural."

"She seems to be fond of you," observed Mr. Stead to Fabio. Ana glared at him but said nothing.

"What about diseases?" said Mr. Stead. "You've had her checked?"

"She was examined by a doctor in Rio. I have the certificate in my car."

"I'd like to make my own visual examination."

"It isn't usual," said Cesar after a pause.

"Perhaps not, but you're charging a very high fee for this adoption."

"I've every right to. Look at her. Look at that skin."

"Very nice, yes, but she's not unique."

"Oh well," Cesar shrugged. "If you don't like her there are plenty who will. And who can afford it."

"I'm not questioning the fee. I just want a quick inspection, that's all. Surely that's not too much to ask? Unless there's something to hide?"

"Of course there's nothing to hide." Cesar took the resisting child from Fabio and put her down on the cot, where Ana undressed her quickly. Mr. Stead's eyes darted over her. He placed his fingertips on the small shoulderblades and ran them down the silk skin of the back, over the already girlish waist to the round buttocks. He grunted. He turned the child over—she began to kick furiously—glanced, was satisfied.

As Ana slipped the dress on again, Cesar said to Fabio, "Bring her over tomorrow morning in the pickup. Tell Mario to let you have the petrol."

3

The washbasins at the Hotel Aurora were almost too small to get your hands in, and the mirror on this occasion had all four corners missing. However, the room was clean and naturally he did not intend to sleep in the bed. The place was useful.

It did have one serious disadvantage. The electric light was so feeble that applying make-up was extremely difficult, particularly as all the mirrors were cracked, broken or covered in fungoid spots. Each time, Roberto made a mental note that next time he must bring his own lightbulb. It was probably as well that he always forgot. Inspection of the light-fittings suggested that any tinkering with them might plunge the entire building into darkness.

Normally Roberto shunned the low-class and dingy. He had come from poverty, and he had a deep fear, which surfaced in his dreams, that one day he would find himself back in it and discover he had not been absent. But on his night-time excursions in female dress he broke his rule. It was partly from necessity. In the kind of hotel he preferred to stay in, he would not be able to do what he was doing now. And in time he had developed a fondness for the Hotel Aurora, where nobody asked questions and which, after several visits, had accumulated several agreeable memories. Such hotels, too, were situated in the parts of town to which, on these occasions, he felt drawn. He liked to walk in the alleys where the prostitutes stood, one hand on hip. How they watched him. He liked to feel them watching him. That steely, silky stare. They took him for a woman, of course, and were afraid of competition, although they should be able to tell from the quality of his clothes and the way he wore them that he was not one of their number. But he thought that they also subconsciously responded to him as a man. Once, being careful to explain himself as he made the approach, he had taken one back to his hotel. It was a disaster, a shaming débâcle. The woman spoiled it: that was the only way he could put it in his mind. He had never tried again, although he continued to resort to prostitutes on other occasions. It was as if, when he dressed, he became his own woman, and must not look for another. Certainly he felt desire towards himself. He did not understand this.

He stood under the meager bulb in the odd-shaped room with its barred window. He stood naked, looking in the mirror. It showed him his face. Always, before he began, Roberto Bandeira studied his face, to see what it contained. He had never grown any better at deciphering it. Sometimes his face seemed completely strange to him, but whether it was too familiar to be articulate or too strange to be read, it was equally inscrutable. So, having tried and failed to understand it, he then looked at it as a face that might or might not be beautiful.

What was beauty? He saw it in a landscape sometimes, although landscape did not much interest him;

he saw it in certain things whose quality was speed: a horse, a boat, a car. But principally beauty was for him a female attribute. He did not think that men possessed it to any important degree, or that it was proper to think of men in such terms. (He hated homosexuals.) When he looked for beauty in his face, therefore, it was for something having a quality of the feminine that he looked. He found it, he thought, in a fullness of the mouth and a lustrousness of the eyes, both of which he would seek to accentuate with make-up.

It was time to begin. He drew from the suitcase a pair of lace-trimmed knickers in peach silk. He had bought them in São Paulo and they were the most expensive item of the outfit, except for the shoes, and he had had to go to a theatrical costumier for those. As the silk touched him he drew in his breath. He was always tempted to stop at this point, go no further, because compared with this moment everything that happened later was almost a disappointment. But he knew that if he did not go on, there would be no point in what he had so far done. He must go out and show himself.

He picked up the padded brassière. He had felt ashamed the first time he put it on: it brought him back to his ugliness. Now he thought of it differently. It was a part of his other self, not a deception. It was really *him*. He fastened the hooks—not easy, he ought to sew on bigger hooks, but he didn't know how—and cupped his hands on it, stirred.

The tights irritated him. He did not see why things had to be so difficult. They were always too small, and however he tried to roll them on he usually ended up pulling holes in them.

The dress. This one was dark blue with elbow-length sleeves (uncomfortably tight, but he could put up with that for a couple of hours) and a white belt. It was very smart. He wondered if perhaps the hemline was a bit high—he didn't want to give the wrong impression, didn't want to look as if he was out to seduce—but he decided that it wasn't, that the important thing was the walk. He was fairly confident of his walk: he had taken much trouble over it. He lifted the blue dress out of its tissue paper, carefully. With care, hardly breathing, he put it on, wriggling patiently into the too-tight armholes and tugging down the bodice, which wanted to stay too high up. Should he wear a corset? He fastened the dress with clumsy fingers, for a moment hating himself.

He turned again to the suitcase and took out the wig. He was pleased with the wig: he had bought it in a shop that sold paraphernalia for the *macumba* rites, so he had been able to try it on. He placed it on his head and turned to the mirror. Seriously, he considered the face crowned with its russet curls.

Yes.

He removed the wig and, with a quickening of the heart, because this was the culmination, this was the very statement, he began to make up his face. He dipped his finger into the little pot of cream—how delicious, that coolness on his fingertip—and leaned forward, rapt.

He stepped out of the hotel doorway forty minutes later, Roberto Bandeira in the guise of a woman, believing himself indistinguishable from a woman and superior to many in his grooming and taste, a man who despised women but had no inkling of it.

TEN

1

The road ran between red banks of soil deeply eroded by old water channels. At the top of the banks some thin, dry grass clung to life. When it rained the water would cascade down the banks and wash great lumps of soil into the road. It was hard to imagine. When it hadn't rained for so long, you forgot what rain was like. It was funny, that, thought Fabio.

You forgot a lot of things when they weren't happening. You forgot the feeling of being trapped, how it began with rage and ended with numbness. You forgot how certain smells could make you despair.

He drove steadily, holding the rattling pick-up at a speed which was as fast as he dared take it and approximately two-thirds of the speed he would like to be doing. The driver's seat had been badly repaired by Mario: it was too near the ground and he was afraid to lean back with his full weight in it in case he detached the back altogether (or even the base, which he fancied had moved a fraction when he braked at a crossroads). The state of the suspension filled him with dread and he avoided thinking about it.

It was still quite early: he had left the farm at eight. Through the permanently half-open driver's window the clean air of the highlands gusted in. This was picturesque country. Hummocky, pleated hills dropped steeply to shadowed valleys dotted with farmsteads. The farms were wooden buildings on stilts, with terracotta roofs that glowed peachy-orange against the forest greenery. Smoke rose from the chimneys. In the valleys cows ambled; here and there was a horse. The road, curving round the sides of the hills, indulged in dizzying bends and steep gradients. Some of the bends, where the drop was precipitous, were fenced, some weren't; cars had gone over whether there was a fence in the way or not.

Fabio took these bends with care, but also with a certain pleasure. He was a good driver and enjoyed his own skill, and although he would have preferred to be driving Cesar's red Volkswagen he was deriving much satisfaction from managing the vagaries of the pickup, with its catankerous gearbox and uncertain steering. He was aware that this pleasure would not last the journey.

There had been little traffic so far: mostly long-distance lorries. The occasional very expensive, very fast car. The occasional very slow, heavily laden farm truck. Traffic would build up as he approached Rio. He scanned the horizon and saw on the edge of the sky the familiar yellowish stain. Another hour, perhaps more. Cesar was not expecting him until twelve o'clock. It was now nine-thirty. The farm had no telephone.

The crevices in the red soil were like faces. They were ugly but not unfriendly. He made a face back.

On the feeder road an hour and ten minutes later, deafened by lorry traffic and with the van rocking in the slipstream, he moved over a lane to be ready. It was then he became afraid. He concentrated on an image of the van as a train running on tracks it couldn't leave. He kept his hands still on the wheel.

Then it was done. The road had forked. To his left, increasingly distant, the lorries thundered on towards Rio. His route curved away in a graceful sweep ahead of him.

Three hours later he was obsessed with petrol. He had filled up the tank from Mario's jerricans and had managed to stow an extra one behind the seat, which soon he would need to use. When that petrol was gone, he didn't know what he would do. He was almost out of money. He had thought about this before setting off, and told himself that a solution would occur to him.

Filling up at a petrol station and driving off without paying was a possible solution, but he didn't think it was a very good one. Abandoning the van was another solution, but it was a last resort.

The trouble was, he didn't know how to steal a car. A locked one, that is. He had somehow never learnt. He didn't know which wires to cross under the bonnet, and he didn't fancy trying to find out in circumstances as stressful as these were.

He glanced again at the petrol gauge. It was practically the only thing in the vehicle you could rely on, and it said Empty.

There was a café up ahead: the usual low, tin-roofed shack with a jumble of chairs in the dust, that would sell five or six different kinds of cane spirit and

a few reheated savouries. He pulled in, and then saw
that what had appeared to be one shack was a line of
three—the café, a rudimentary grocery shop and a hut
that sold vehicle spares. Fabio investigated the third.
The motor parts were covered in a film of oily dust
and neither they nor the boy on the stool looked as if
they wanted to be disturbed. Fabio was about to walk
out again when something caught his eye, and he
bought it without even asking the price: a length of
plastic tubing.

He gulped some coffee, and in the shop bought
biscuits, mineral water and bananas. He refilled the
petrol tank from Mario's jerrican, and after another
ten minutes or so was ready to drive on.

The roads approaching São Paulo were choked
with rush-hour traffic. It took him an hour and a half
to battle past the city, anxiously eyeing the tempera-
ture gauge, and get on the coast road. Then he had to
stop at the next service station. He took the opportunity to stretch his legs and eat some biscuits and
bananas. It was getting dark.

An hour later, when it was properly dark, he
turned off the road into a sleepy little town. After some
reconnoitering he found what he wanted: an unat-
tended taxi on a parking lot screened by buildings. It
took him only a few minutes to siphon out the petrol
and get away.

At eight o'clock he ate some more biscuits, shifted
his position yet again to ease the ache in his back, and
realized he had been driving for twelve hours. He had
grossly miscalculated the time it would take. He had
thought he could do it in a day. He was going to have
to stop soon.

Two hours later the advancing headlights were
drilling into his eyes and leaving them dazzled for the

road that came after. His head felt very heavy. He closed his eyes for a moment to rest them.

His head was so heavy he didn't know how he could keep holding it up.

He came to himself just in time to pull the van away before it crossed into the oncoming headlights. A lorry's horn blared into the night behind him. Shaken, Fabio dropped his speed and began to look for a place to stop.

Where a village was signposted he turned off and, after a short distance on the winding road, noticed a quarry cut into the hill. He drove into it, and, switching off the engine, was stunned by the silence.

He got out to stretch his cramped muscles. The night was brilliant with stars and—he could now hear—clamorous with insects. A firefly darted in front of him. A horse champed somewhere.

Fabio checked his watch, got back in the van and fell asleep as soon as he closed his eyes.

2

Sergio had the feeling that he was being watched. It had started when he drew up in his Beetle at the wrought-iron gates. As instructed, he got out and pressed a bell in the wall, and after a moment the gates opened. He drove through and they shut behind him. The house was a hundred yards down the drive. He saw a movement of leaves in the shrubbery as he passed it, and a curtain twitched in one of the upper windows.

It was a large house, built within the past ten years. The basic design was simple: a two-story, L-shaped building under a tiled roof, arched windows

of generous width with wooden shutters, a stone path
leading to a plain, dignified front door. The impression
of solidity was strengthened by the thickness of the
walls which was visible at the window apertures, and
by the bronze gratings that protected the lower windows. A verandah ran right round the house. An arch-
way in the wall to the right of the main door led into
a garden or courtyard, from which came women's
voices. At the back of the house the land sloped away.
There would be a view across the valley.

To this pleasant architectural concept the owner
had added touches of his own: a lily pond crossed by
an ornamental bridge and containing an island on
which was set a pagoda; a dovecote; a windmill; a
sundial.

Sergio parked by the sundial, and walked to the
front door where a painted wooden Negro stood in
attendance. He knocked with the brass knocker.

Bandeira himself opened the door.

His manner conveyed a barely controlled impatience. "Yes, come in. I'm afraid I haven't got long."

Sergio followed him across a parquet-floored hall
and through two large reception rooms in which
French windows opened on to a lawn kept green by
sprinklers.

Bandeira turned into a tiled passageway, opened
a door and stood back for Sergio to enter. He waved a
hand at a leather-and-chrome chair.

Sergio sat down.

"Cigarette?"

"No, thank you. I don't smoke."

Bandeira took one from an onyx box and lit it with
a gold lighter. He sat with his elbows on the huge
empty desk, hands clasped at the level of his chin, the
cigarette looking fragile between his laced fingers.

"What can I do for you?"

It had cost Sergio a lot to ask for this interview, to insist on it in the face of Bandeira's reluctance, and to come here. It had involved disregarding Rosa's quite explicit wishes. He believed it had to be done. He knew Rosa. She was impulsive, and sometimes she regretted things. He would not stand by and watch her impulsively throw her future away.

"We have something of mutual interest to discuss," said Sergio.

"So you said. I don't know you. I don't see what mutual interest we can have."

"Does the name Rosa Van Meurs mean anything to you?"

Bandeira's features seemed to expand in surprise. "Rosa Van Meurs," he repeated. Then, "Oh yes. School-teacher. I visited the school. Pretty girl." An insinuating smile appeared on his lips. "Is she a friend of yours?"

"Yes, she is."

Bandeira laughed. "All right, I took her out to lunch. It's a free country, a man can buy lunch for a pretty girl. I haven't been fingering your goods, and if I had I'd tell you you were a damn fool not to keep a closer eye on them. Is that all you came to see me about?"

Sergio said he didn't care who Bandeira took out to lunch, he was concerned with threats, anonymous letters and blackmail.

There was a pause in which Bandeira visibly deployed his forces. Then he said evenly, "What on earth are you talking about?"

"In the past two months you've been carrying on a campaign of intimidation against Rosa Van Meurs," said Sergio. "It began with an anonymous letter, con-

tinued with the visit of a school inspector who threatened her with the loss of her job—"

"Really, I've no idea what you're talking about."

"—and culminated in your attempt to blackmail
her into a deal. She could have her job back in return
for keeping quiet about something you're doing in the
Pantanal."

"Rubbish. Absolute rubbish. You'd better leave
now."

"I have no intention of leaving."

"Then I shall ask the servants—"

"You've been up to some pretty dirty tricks, Mr.
Bandeira, and I intend to bring them to full public
notice unless I—"

"Oh, do you?" said Roberto Bandeira. "And how
far do you think you'll get, when you can't prove anything at all except that, as you say, I offered to do a
deal with her? I don't know what you do for a living
but you obviously don't know much about the real
world. That's how business is conducted."

"I know how business is conducted," said Sergio. "I
deal with industrialists every week. They poison the
rivers and pollute the seas and talk about economic
imperatives, but most of them would draw the line at
hounding a woman out of her job and threatening to
wash her mouth out with acid."

He saw Bandeira flinch, but on the heavy face
opposite him he saw no surprise.

"I don't know anything about threats of that sort."

"I think otherwise," said Sergio, adding, with
inspiration, "and so do the police."

"The police?" But after a second Bandeira leapt
on it. "Then why don't they arrest me? You can't go
round making threats against people with impunity."

Why, indeed? It had not been an inspiration. It exposed the essential weakness of Sergio's position.

"I don't think they can be very sure of their ground," smiled Bandeira. "You know, on the whole the police prefer not to make fools of themselves."

"Are you suggesting that a man in your position can afford to ignore the police?"

Bandeira flicked ash from his cigarette. "A man in my position is certainly not going to be arrested on the strength of some wild allegation," he said. "What evidence have you got that I made these threats?"

"You think you can buy anyone, don't you?"

"Are you saying that I've bought the police?"

It seemed to Sergio that he had already lost whatever grip he'd had on the interview.

"What *do* you do for a living, by the way?"

"I'm a marine biologist."

"Yes, I might have known you were something like that. Well, let me give you a piece of information which you won't find lying about in your laboratory. Most people can be bought, and a lot of them can hardly wait to be."

"You didn't succeed in buying Rosa, though, did you?"

"There was no attempt to buy her. It was a business proposal. She's an obstinate young lady."

Sergio sat back in his chair. It represented several months' wages for a laboratory assistant. He made himself think calmly.

"So you found Rosa obstinate?" he said. "She's certainly strong-minded."

"She'll do herself no good that way," said Bandeira.

"That seems to be what you told her."

"I mean generally. It's not an attractive thing in a woman."

ANTA MASON

"Oh, I see. You must have been surprised by her refusal to budge. You went to a lot of trouble, didn't you?"

"What d'you mean by that?"

"Or perhaps you didn't; perhaps that so-called inspector wasn't from the Ministry at all, just someone you met in a bar?"

"Of course he was from the Ministry," said Bandeira irritably.

"Ah. So you were behind his visit to the school?"

"If I happened to know about it, what difference does it make?"

"You must have a lot of contacts."

Bandeira was not a subtle man.

"I have many contacts, including some in very high places." He put out his cigarette in the onyx ashtray. "That inspector is my wife's brother." A touch of pride invaded his voice. "He's tipped to go a long way."

Sergio, despite his anger, was fascinated, and felt a little surge of triumph at having so simply elicited the truth.

"So, you see, you have nothing to make a fuss about," said Bandeira. "It's not a crime to have a brother-in-law employed by the Ministry of Education, and it's not a crime to have a conversation with him."

And if it were a crime, thought Sergio, who would call him to account for it, and would not every word of that conversation be denied?

His exhilaration of a moment ago evaporated. Disgust and defeat swept over him together. He was tempted to stand up and take his leave and go and walk for hours along the beaches until the taste of this encounter faded from his mind. He fought off the defeat: it was what Bandeira was counting on.

"But it doesn't look very pretty, does it?" he persisted. "A man in your position, victimizing a woman. A man hoping to be elected to the town council, what's more. It wouldn't help you much, if it became common gossip."

"Are you trying to blackmail me?"

Sergio let the question hang in the air for a few moments before he said, "And all for what? For the sake of something which is illegal in the first place."

"What nonsense. The gold mine is licensed by the government."

"The road across the Indian reserve isn't."

"What road across an Indian reserve?" said Bandeira. "Our road is perfectly legitimate. Nobody has studied the maps. Water-courses change all the time in the Pantanal. Naturally that affects boundaries. Our road is legal and Funai is going to say so."

Sergio had, for the first time in that interview, to hold down real rage.

"Particularly," continued Bandeira, "as we have a letter from Dr. Van Meurs in support of our case."

"Dr.—"

"Rosa's father."

Shock kept Sergio silent for a time. But there was no need to say anything. He could see how it had been done. A visit to the old Indianist, his wits wandering, his address easily obtained from Rosa . . . Oh, poor Rosa.

"So, as it turns out, I don't need your girlfriend's cooperation," said Bandeira.

He began opening the drawers of his desk in an unhurried way, looking for something. Eventually he found it: a box of cigars. He took a long time over selecting one, sniffing it, and lighting it, which had to be done with a box of matches from the other side of the room and not with the gold lighter. He inhaled the smoke with obvious pleasure.

Then he said, "So I suppose I could do her a favor. But I don't think I will."

"Why not, if it costs you nothing?"

"Why should I?" said Bandeira. "She wasn't very polite to me, you know."

About a minute went by. Then Sergio said, "If you continue with your petty vengeance you'll oblige me to resort to the same methods as you use."

Bandeira laughed. "You can't hurt me. You think you can damage my reputation by repeating the fantasies of some neurotic schoolteacher? Say what you like to whom you like. D'you know how much you'll cost me in votes?" He snapped his fingers in the air. "That much."

"I wasn't thinking of telling people that you're a bully and a petty criminal," said Sergio. "I was thinking of telling them that you like to dress rather strangely from time to time."

The silence was terrible.

Then: "Dress—?" said Bandeira.

Abruptly, he stood up and went to the cocktail bar, where, with his back to Sergio, he made a great show of running his fingers along the bottles. "Drink?" he asked without turning round.

"No, thank you."

Bandeira poured himself a whisky and stood with it in his hand, looking out of the window. Eventually he said, "What did you mean by that remark?"

Sergio said, "You're a transvestite, Mr. Bandeira." He said it quite gently, which surprised him.

He had never before seen a man's face collapse. It crumpled and became old. This was not a thing that should be watched. Sergio watched it a fraction too long before he looked away.

Bandeira walked to a chair and sat down in it. He stared in front of him, seeing nothing. Then, at last, he saw Sergio, and the look he gave him Sergio never forgot. Receiving that look and understanding in that moment that Rosa had been right, Sergio felt something crumble inside him and experienced a powerful impulse to say he was sorry. He crushed it furiously. Humanity would ruin everything.

"So," said Roberto Bandeira. "You know this." He tilted his glass from side to side, watching the movement of the liquid. "No one would believe you."

"I think they would."

"Do you?"

"It sounds so unlikely, people would think there had to be some truth in it."

Bandeira said nothing.

"In any case," said Sergio, "there are already some people who know. And when the story gets into the papers, they'll come out of the woodwork."

He felt intense distaste for what he was saying, but not all of him felt it.

"People of no account," said Bandeira. He swigged his whisky.

"People of no account can do you quite a lot of harm," said Sergio. "Don't despise them. They're where you came from."

The part of Sergio that did not feel distaste for what he was doing was quite enjoying it.

"It doesn't matter whether people believe it or not," he continued. "The effect on your life is what matters. The reporters on the doorstep . . . what will your family say? The laughter that suddenly stops when you enter a room. Or suddenly starts. Your fellow directors . . . You'll never get into politics, of course. How can you? You'll never dare to address a public meeting for fear of what some wit will shout at you."

Bandeira stood up. He had himself in hand again.

"What's your price?"

"Rosa Van Meurs keeps her job. Call off your brother-in-law."

"What makes you think I can do that at this stage?"

"Well, if you can't there's no deal," said Sergio.

Bandeira gave him almost a snarl, with lips drawn back.

"You're taking a risk, aren't you? If I'm the sort of character you think I am?"

"This isn't Bolivia," said Sergio. "Pick up that phone and call your tame inspector, and let's get it over with."

He felt dirty. He felt exhausted. He also felt oddly excited, and although he was longing to get out of the house something in him would not have minded lingering there.

Bandeira, lowering himself into the chair behind the desk, said suddenly, and as if driven to it, "Have you seen me?" He hesitated. "Dressed?"

Sergio tensed. "I saw you in Cuiabá."

"But surely you didn't recognize me? Surely, when I'm . . . when I'm like that, I don't look . . ."

Sergio understood something and could not restrain his cruelty. "You don't look like a woman," he said. "How can you imagine that you do? You look grotesque."

3

The landscape was careless, sprawling and patient. It made Fabio think of some huge, tawny animal.

He had left the hills into which the road took him on the second day, but he could see them in the distance, a hummocky bluish line nudging up into the purer blue of the sky. A file of white herons beat the air ahead of him. There must be water near.

He passed veranda-ed houses with red-tiled roofs half-hidden by the great fringed, paddle-like leaves of banana trees. He passed small green plantations— mango, papaya, tamarind, a patch of coffee, a rough shack—tended by men who themselves looked like a part of the earth. He saw dogs, bony cattle, five children on a bicycle, and a wrecked bus at the bottom of a bank which someone had turned into a goatshed.

He had slept little, and the brilliant clarity of the light seemed to him to have a hallucinatory quality, so that, in the moment of seeing something, he knew he was seeing it, but he was not sure he had seen it a moment later. The same hallucinatory clarity seemed to be inside his skull, into which thoughts came, discrete and fashioned like cut stones, and then disappeared without trace, leaving him wondering what he could have been thinking about for several hours.

He didn't have the faintest idea what he was going to do after he had seen Rosa. He would have to go away again at once. Where?

But it would be all right. Hadn't it been all right so far?

The land to his left dipped away and he saw the blaze of the sea.

Happiness surged over him and he had to make a real effort to go on driving sensibly instead of doing something crazy with the steering wheel.

4

It was Sergio's birthday. Rosa had bought him a watch, to replace the one he had had since he was a schoolboy, to which he obstinately clung although it was now unreliable. He said you couldn't get a good quartz watch with a second hand, and he refused to consider a digital watch because he said they were ugly.

Rosa had found, by diligent searching, a Japanese quartz watch which had a second hand, a pleasing appearance and several other useful qualities. It was horribly expensive, but it was for Sergio.

He was coming to collect her at eight, and they were going out to dinner. Sergio had booked a table at a new restaurant called Senzala. lt was a *churrascaria*, where the waiters brought cuts of charcoal-grilled meat to your table and you could eat as much as you wanted. Rosa preferred to avoid these places because she always ate too much and felt awful afterwards, but Sergio liked them and it was Sergio's birthday.

Rosa sighed as she dressed and inspected herself in the mirror. The evening was to be enjoyed, but the thought of it weighed on her like lead. It was partly, she supposed, that she was worried about Fabio. He had been gone for a week and she had heard nothing. He was inconsiderate, but he would surely have been in touch with her by now if he was able to. He knew

Marcia's telephone number; he could have left a message. Fabio is dead, her mind said. She turned away from the mirror, having glimpsed the skull behind her own face.

Sergio arrived ten minutes later, bearing champagne.

"Heavens!" said Rosa. "What are we going to drink it out of?"

"Oh, anything," said Sergio, who seemed happy but preoccupied.

Rosa presented the watch. She had wrapped it beautifully. Sergio, an orderly person, enjoyed the game of unwrapping it without tearing the paper. He stared at the watch, and smiled slowly.

"Rosa, it's beautiful. Thank you."

"It has a second hand."

"So it has. And a—how shall I put it—a look of restrained elegance."

"As befits a marine biologist."

"Quite so."

"It's waterproof."

"Is it? Wonderful, I can mess about in the lab in it."

"I'm not sure it's plankton-proof."

"Oh, it will be. The Japanese are very clever."

They sat close together on the sofa and drank champagne. They talked about inconsequential things. Rosa wanted to talk about her visit to her father and the letter he appeared to have signed, but didn't. She thought Sergio had probably heard enough about Indians and Roberto Bandeira. She sensed a peculiar nervousness in him, or perhaps it was an excitement he was holding back that was making him jumpy. Whatever it was, it was uncharacteristic. She lacked the energy to ask him. The champagne, the first sips of which had lifted her spirits, was after a glassful having the opposite effect. She shook her head when Sergio tried to refill her glass.

"You look sad," he said.

"I'm worried about Fabio."

"You still haven't heard anything?"

"No."

"You think he's been kidnapped by this Cesar character?" Rosa had filled him in to some extent on Fabio's background, but Sergio had never really believed in Cesar. Fabio had a vivid imagination, he said.

"What other explanation is there? People don't just disappear."

"What about the place where he worked?"

"It's locked up. The priest's never there."

"Perhaps you should go to Mass. He'd have to be there for that."

"It isn't a joke, Sergio."

"I'm sorry," said Sergio contritely. "Poor little Fabio. You got quite fond of him, didn't you?"

"Yes."

"He got quite fond of you, as well."

"What d'you mean?" frowned Rosa.

"Mmm, I didn't think you'd noticed. Well, it probably did him good. Anyway, there isn't anything you can do, is there?"

"Nothing at all."

"Well, then. Let's go and have dinner."

He stood up.

"I feel it's my fault," said Rosa miserably.

"How on earth is it your fault?"

"I made him go out."

"What?"

Rosa explained about Fabio's reluctance to leave the flat.

Sergio said, "You mean you should have allowed

him to shut himself up in this flat like some frightened animal? For ever?"

"I suppose I couldn't have."

"Of course you couldn't. You did what any sensible person would have done, and you did it in his own interests. It was very generous of you to let him stay here at all."

"That doesn't seem particularly relevant."

"There's nothing we can do," said Sergio with emphasis. "Let us, therefore, with all due respect to Fabio, forget about him and go and celebrate my birthday."

"Yes, let's," said Rosa. "I'm sorry."

He drew her to her feet. In his face there was a mixture of tenderness, hesitancy and—she thought—triumph. An odd mixture.

"What is it?" she asked.

"What is what?"

"You've got something to tell me which you think I might not like. But you're pleased about it. Yes?"

"You never miss," said Sergio. "I was waiting for the right moment."

"Sergio, you're hopeless. You are quite transparent."

She was certain that whatever the news was, she would be pleased if he was pleased. "Let me guess. You've been offered the directorship of a laboratory in—um—Salvador, at three times your present salary, and I shall only see you three times a year."

Sergio looked stunned. "No. And I must say the prospect of only seeing me three times a year doesn't seem to dismay you very much."

Oh dear, thought Rosa.

"Of course it would dismay me. What is it, then?"

He backed away a little, as if he needed to put a distance between them.

He said, "The champagne is to celebrate the return of Rosa to the teaching profession. There will be a letter on your headmaster's desk tomorrow, saying that the objections to your teaching have been withdrawn."

The room spun round Rosa. Joy and relief fought with a terrible suspicion. But she could not believe that Sergio had betrayed her. Not Sergio.

With a forced calm, she said, "How do you know?"

She saw that he was forcing himself to be calm as well. "I went to see Roberto Bandeira yesterday."

"Sergio!" It was a plea.

He half-turned away. "We had quite a long conversation. He is completely without scruples, of course." Sergio inspected his fingernails fastidiously. "He began by denying everything and saying that it was no crime to take a pretty woman out to lunch, and ended by more or less admitting being behind the letter and the inspector's visit and saying what was I going to do about it? The police don't come into it, of course. The inspector is his brother-in-law, by the way."

Rosa was staring at him.

"He said I couldn't prove anything and that I didn't know anything about the real world." Sergio gave a short laugh. "He also gave me the line about that wretched road of his not being on Indian land."

"It sounds as if he had you running by the end."

"He did," Sergio admitted.

"So how did you manage . . . ?" She weighed him up as he stood there, nervous, defensive, proud, the one man she had completely trusted. "How did you manage to change his mind?"

Sergio did not reply.

"You blackmailed him," she said flatly.

Sergio sat down on a chair, looking tired. "Yes," he said, "I did."

"You threatened to expose him as a transvestite."

"Yes."

"It isn't even illegal."

"I know."

"How ironic," said Rosa.

She began to walk around the room, absently tidying things. Sergio watched her with a helpless expression. After a while he said, "Rosa—"

She waved away the sound of his voice. She wanted to be alone.

"Rosa, it has saved your job."

"I told you not to do it."

"Yes, I know. I'm sorry. I know it was . . . I didn't know what else to do."

"Why do anything?" asked Rosa bitterly.

"For you. I wanted to help you."

"You did this for me?"

"Yes!"

"In spite of what I said?"

He was silent.

Rosa shouted at him, *"How dare you?"*

He flinched away from her fury and sat, white and tense, with his hands resting on the dining table.

"You haven't done something *for* me, you've done something *to* me," Rosa said. "You overruled a decision *I* had made, about something which concerned me alone, *in my interests*. What on earth do you think gave you the right to do that? The fact that I'm a woman?"

"That's ridiculous."

"It's the only explanation I can see."

"For heaven's sake," said Sergio, grasping in desperation at the worst thing he could have said, "does it really matter that much?"

She stared at him. If he thought it didn't matter, what was there to say?

"You've involved me in something I find horrible and can't now disengage myself from," she said. "That's the other thing you've done to me. You wouldn't accept my decision but I have to live with yours. Blackmailing a man over a harmless quirk he's ashamed of."

Sergio said, as he had said before, "But he is Roberto Bandeira."

Rosa went to the sofa and sat down. "I don't know how to get through to you," she said.

She saw with complete clarity that they did not understand one another and that at the deepest level they would work against each other. He had trapped her in his decision, done it "for her," and did not know why it mattered so much. He would do the same again. And if she tried to tell him this, he would not know what she meant.

"I don't think we have anything in common," she said. It was a quiet statement, made almost to herself.

"Rosa!" In passionate protest Sergio brought his hand down on the table. "What are you *talking* about?"

She watched him from a great distance, feeling his distress, herself paralyzed. Something irrevocable had happened.

5

Fabio mounted the steps to Rosa's flat. They were stone steps, and quite high, but he took them slowly. One step at a time. That's the way.

As he neared the top and saw again the familiar door, his sureness that he had done the right thing suddenly evaporated, leaving him apprehensive. She had been quite definite on this subject. He had thought she didn't mean it. People often didn't know their own minds.

And what else could he have done?

He rang the bell.

After an interval Rosa, unusually pale, came to the door.

She looked, at first with incomprehension, and then with disbelief, at the man, blinking with tiredness, and the little girl who held his hand.